M000190799

She's Missing

Mike Paull

A Wings ePress, Inc.
Spy Thriller Novel

Wings ePress, Inc.

Edited by: Jeanne Smith
Copy Edited by: Brian Hatfield
Executive Editor: Jeanne Smith
Cover Artist: Trisha FitzGerald-Jung
Woman Image by Darina Belonga from Pexels
Jerusalem by Sosinda from Pixabay

All rights reserved

Names, characters and incidents depicted in this book are products of the author's imagination or are used fictitiously. Any resemblance to actual events, locales, organizations, or persons, living or dead, is entirely coincidental and beyond the intent of the author or the publisher.

No part of this book may be reproduced or transmitted in any form or by any means, electronic or mechanical, including photocopying, recording, or by any information storage and retrieval system, without permission in writing from the publisher.

Wings ePress Books
www.wingsepress.com

Copyright © 2022 by: Mike Paull
ISBN-13: 978-1-61309-975-9
ISBN-10: 1-61309-975-4

Published In the United States Of America

Wings ePress Inc.
3000 N. Rock Road
Newton, KS 67114

What They Are Saying About
She's Missing

She's Missing, by Mike Paull, is a rip-roaring spy yarn that starts fast and accelerates from there. Fast action, accurate geopolitical settings, and full dimensional characters make *She's Missing* a compelling story ripped out of today's headlines. It's a page burner that will keep the reader up all night trying to finish.

> --Jamie Dodson, award winning author of the
> Nick Grant Adventure series

Paull's twisty tale and propulsive action unwind a cagey deception as Coop and friends "follow the money." From spy craft to aircraft and a nail-biting trip into Iran, the novel keeps readers in suspense until the last, bittersweet page.

> —Dan Barnett, book columnist, Chico (CA)
> *Enterprise-Record*

This second-in-a series spy thriller from Mike Paull proves that creativity and imagination are alive and well. *She's Missing,* like the book before it, mixes intrigue, danger, and unexpected plot twists to keep the reader wondering what will happen next. As the story progresses and the suspense escalates, Mike makes you realize that things are never what they appear. Plan to stay up late reading this one.

> --Nora Profit, award winning writer and founder of
> the Writing Loft

My Thanks

I would like to thank Brad Liebman, my good friend of fifty years, for urging me to create a book two in the *Missing* series. He was relentless, and thankfully I agreed.

I would also like to thank my beta readers: Scott Paulo, Ray Schimmel and Brad Liebman. I followed their suggestions and the finished product reflects much of their hard work and advice.

My thanks to Wings ePress, Inc. It was a pleasure to work again with CEO Linda Voth, Executive Editor Jeanne Smith and their staff.

None of my books would be complete without thanking my wife, Bev. She listened and listened, over and over, to every word change, every sentence change and every paragraph change. Some she agreed with and others she did not. What appears on the following pages is the result of her critiques.

Dedication

To my wonderful wife Bev, who has stood beside me not only through the good times, but also through the bad.

* * *

"When a sinister person means to be your enemy, they always start by trying to become your friend."
—William Blake, 1757-1827

One

The wind whistled across the waters of the Potomac carrying a combination of freezing rain and light snow. Coop glanced at the windows of his fourth-floor office. They were rattling and creaking as the sleet pounded against the bulletproof glass. He ignored the sounds and re-read the memo sent from the director of national intelligence to both the agency director and to him, the deputy director. He zeroed in on the last few words...*in Israel the penalty for espionage or for aiding and abetting the enemy is imprisonment for life.*

Coop's cell phone vibrated. He picked it up to check the caller I.D. and felt his stomach turn a somersault. Every day for over two years now, he had thumbed through his missed calls hoping he would find one from her. The last time he talked to his fellow agent and best friend was before she saved his life and disappeared to Zurich with the nine million dollars the two of them had recovered from an operation in the Middle East. He didn't care about the cash. It was dirty money that only a few people knew about, and besides, it didn't really belong to anyone, let alone the government. What he did care about was her and how she was getting along in Zurich with her new life and her new domestic partner.

He slid his index finger across the iPhone screen and put it to his ear. "Zoe? Is that you?"

There was a pause and then a voice said, "No. No, it is not."

"Well, who is this then?"

"Uh, this is her partner, Lara...Lara Graf."

"Where's Zoe? Is she all right?"

There was another pause, much longer than the first. "That is why I am calling. We are on holiday in Cyprus and...and she... she disappeared."

"What d'ya mean, disappeared?"

"We checked into the hotel in Limassol and Zoe went down to the lobby to talk to the concierge about restaurants. I unpacked, put a few things away and stepped into the shower. When I got out, I realized she had been gone for over an hour and I became concerned, so I called down. The concierge said she never showed up. I did not know who to call, but I knew you were in her phone so...I just did not know who..."

"It's okay, you did the right thing. If you don't hear from her in the next hour, call me back."

"Should I call the police?"

"No, don't do that. This may be something way beyond what the police can handle. Just call me back if you don't hear from her."

He closed his phone and re-read the memo. Coop didn't believe in coincidence—in his job he couldn't afford to. The fact that the national intelligence memo and Zoe's sudden disappearance surfaced on the same day gave him a queasy feeling in his gut and when he followed his gut, he was usually right.

Coop knew that Agency policy was to destroy the memo, but instead he dropped it into his pocket. He grabbed his coat and opened the door to the reception room where his secretary was struggling with a data entry. "I'll be out for the rest of the afternoon," he said and disappeared out the main door. He looked at his watch; it was 2:20. His wife was the scrub nurse for a complex back surgery that had begun three hours earlier. He figured by the time he got to the hospital, she would be either be changing her clothes or just winding down from a stressful morning.

The Virginia Hospital Center was just across the 14th Street Bridge in Arlington. The traffic on I-395 was moving faster than usual and Coop pulled into the hospital parking lot within fifteen minutes after leaving the capital. He headed straight to the surgical post-op ward on the third floor. A gray-haired woman dressed in civilian clothes, who fit the description of a hospital volunteer, looked up from behind a Formica counter. "May I help you?"

Coop took out his wallet, opened it so his gold shield was visible and held it where the woman could see it. "Craig Cooper, Fran Cooper's husband. Is she out of surgery yet?"

The woman held up a finger on her left hand while she typed into a computer with her right. "Yes, it looks like they finished twenty minutes ago. The team is probably in the lounge. You can check it out if you'd like." She pointed toward a set of double doors.

The doors opened automatically and Coop stepped into the hallway where he was hit by that unmistakable telltale hospital smell; a noxious combination of medicaments, Clorox and air freshener. It triggered memories of when he had gone through surgery for the removal of the bullet he had taken in his back while chasing through the Middle East in search of Saddam's gold. The door to the lounge was ajar. He peeked his head around it and saw that Fran was having coffee with two other nurses. "Hey, Fran." he said.

She looked up. "Coop? Is everything all right?"

"Well, sorta. Maybe we can talk in private somewhere?"

3

The other two nurses stepped away from the table and started for the door. "We were just leaving," one said. They let the door close behind them.

"What is it?" Fran asked.

"I think Zoe's in trouble."

"What kind of trouble?"

"I don't know, but she disappeared from her hotel in Cyprus. Her partner, Lara, called me."

Fran leaned back uneasily, her mouth forming a pensive frown. "How long ago?"

Coop looked at the wall clock over the sink that was synchronized to the second with all the other clocks in the hospital. "I'm guessing about three hours by now."

"That's not very long."

Coop took the memo from his pocket and handed it to her. She read it and handed it back. "So, you think this is related?"

Coop stepped to the window and looked off into space. After a minute or two, he turned back toward Fran. "Yeah, I'd bet on it."

"What are you going to do?"

Coop bit at his lower lip. "I'm not sure."

"You want to go to Cyprus, don't you?"

Coop took Fran's hands in his. "I promised you and Josh I'd never go back in the field. I can't break that promise."

"Coop, that was before Zoe saved your life. If it weren't for her, you'd have been dead by a sniper's bullet two years ago. You owe her. I owe her. You have no choice; you have to go."

"I know, but I can't renege on my promise to Josh. I let him down before and I don't want to do it again."

"Look, Coop, Josh has to know he owes Zoe too. He's a teenager now. It's time for him to understand what you do and why you do it."

"Yeah, you're right, but..."

"But what?"

"Fran, I'm only a couple years shy of sixty and I haven't been in the field for two years."

Fran smirked. "After thirty years in the field, you don't forget how to be a spy because of a couple years behind a desk." Coop ran his hand through his hair and scratched the back of his head. "What else?" Fran asked.

"I tried to cover for her, but the director was really pissed off that Zoe disappeared without a face to face with him. She just dropped a resignation letter in the mail. He'll never authorize a rescue mission."

"Do you have to tell him?"

"Not really, but he'll probably figure it out."

"So, why even give a damn, what's the worst that can happen? He finds out, fires you and you take an early retirement."

Coop grinned and planted a big kiss on Fran's lips. "As usual, you're right. Why would I give a damn?"

Two

A cold front had passed through an hour ago and stars were beginning to show in the early evening sky. A black Cadillac Escalade drove to the northwest corner of Dulles International and pulled to a stop in back of Ross Aviation, where a Gulfstream G550, bearing the name *Wainwright Construction-Toledo, Ohio*, was waiting twenty yards away. It was loaded with full fuel, enough to travel 7,700 miles, two thousand more than was needed for the trip to Larnaca International on the island of Cyprus.

The driver held the door open and Coop stepped out. He was carrying a briefcase in his left hand and a duffel was slung over his shoulder. He shook hands with the driver and headed toward the private jet.

He stepped inside unnoticed by the captain and copilot, who were working on the preflight check lists, but the flight attendant who was busy warming food spotted Coop coming through the doorway. She smiled, "Good evening, sir. May I get you something to drink?"

"Oh, hi there, Josie. A water would be fine. Carbonated if you have it." Coop was the only passenger; he took a double-wide seat he knew would later fold into a bed.

When the captain realized Coop was aboard, he slipped out of the cockpit and approached him. "Good evening, sir."

Coop looked up. "Oh, nice to see you again, C.T. You can drop the 'sir' stuff. How's the family?"

"Great...and yours?"

Coop nodded. "Fine, just fine. What have you got for me?"

The pilot pointed to the empty seat next to Coop. Coop patted the soft leather. "Sure, sit."

The captain settled in next to Coop, opened a plastic folder and handed him a computer-generated piece of paper. "Here's our course—pretty much direct. We should be off the ground somewhere around seven-thirty. Cyprus is seven hours ahead of us and the flight time is close to twelve and a half, so I estimate we'll touch-down in Larnaca at close to three in the afternoon local time."

Coop looked at the course. It would take them over the North Atlantic to the coast of Spain, then to the Mediterranean over Sicily and Greece and finally direct to the island of Cyprus. "How's the weather?" Coop asked.

"Not bad. We'll catch up to the cold front that passed through D.C., but at thirty-nine thousand we'll be on top of most of it."

"Sounds good. It's almost seven-fifteen. So, we'll be off in fifteen minutes then?

The captain looked at his watch. "Pretty close, our takeoff slot is actually in seventeen minutes. After we level off, feel free to come up front whenever you like." He headed back to the cockpit.

The flight attendant offered Coop dinner, but he wasn't hungry. He reclined the seat all the way and fell asleep. When he awoke, he looked at his Rolex—a welcome home present from Fran—it was 2:30 a.m. D.C. time. He fiddled with the buttons, set it to 9:30 a.m. and did a little math—five and half hours to Cyprus.

Coop caught the eye of the flight attendant, who filled a glass with ice water, scurried over and set it on the worktable in front of him. "I'll bet you're hungry now," she said.

"Yeah, I'm famished. What's in the galley?"

"That depends. Steak if you want dinner; an omelet if you want breakfast."

"How 'bout an omelet and a Jack Daniels—no ice."

She laughed. "I thought I'd seen it all, but that's a first. Do you want them together?"

"No, just bring me the drink and I'll get the food after a shower."

Coop stepped into the bathroom with his carry-on in one hand and the Jack in the other. It was much fancier than his master bath back home. The floor was marble and everything else was granite. He set his drink on the counter and took some shaving supplies from a nearby cabinet. Before removing his two-day growth, he stood back and looked into the mirror. Although he had gone through chemo for lung cancer and lost all his hair, it had returned as thick as before. The only major change was the color; once sandy-brown it was now almost totally gray. He flipped on the water, stood under the shower head and let it wash away what was left of Washington D.C.

After finishing his omelet, Coop made his way to the flight deck. The copilot was monitoring the autopilot and the captain was eating breakfast. "Hey, C.T., how're we doing?" Coop asked.

The captain looked at the GPS display. "Hey, Coop, we're doin' great. We picked up twenty knots on our tail, so we'll be there a half hour early. The coast will be coming up in less than an hour. You'll be able to see Spain off the right wing and France off the left."

"I'll check it out." He glanced at the copilot and tilted his head toward the door. "Listen, C.T., can we talk in private?'

The captain set down his tray. "Sure, let's step out of the cockpit."

C.T. whispered something to the copilot and followed Coop into the hallway. "What's with all this secret stuff? Am I being promoted to Spy First Class?"

"No, don't worry, but after we get there, I'll need you to hang around and be on call for a while."

"Sure, that's no big deal."

"Well, I may need you to do a little tap dancing if Director Dutton's secretary contacts you."

"I'm not sure I know what you mean."

"I don't want anyone to know I'm over here."

"Really? And that includes the director?"

"Especially the director."

C.T.'s face paled. "Coop, we've been friends since we were kids and I wouldn't even have this job if you hadn't pulled some strings, but if I get canned, I don't know what I'll..."

Coop cut him off. "If any shit hits the fan, I'll take the fall. All you have to say is, Deputy Director Cooper ordered me to... you know, whatever."

"How long?"

"Maybe two or three weeks...four max."

C.T. stared off in the distance while he ran the scenario through in his head. "I'm scheduled to fly Dutton and his wife to Florida on Christmas eve. Can you wind up your operation by then?"

"I'll try. I promise."

"Okay, Coop, you're the boss."

"I'll make this up to you, C.T. Thanks."

Coop returned to his seat and opened his briefcase. The memo from the director of national intelligence was on top of all his other papers. He read it again.

*TS/NF/ORCON 22–November-2010–08:22
hours: Intelligence sources indicate that in
response to a recent provocation from an
Iranian-linked operative, Israel has dispatched
Mossad agents to apprehend anyone suspected
of aiding, abetting or spying for Iran. It should
be noted that an individual with possible ties to
a major U.S. intelligence agency is suspected
of being a major player and is being sought by
Mossad. It should also be noted that in Israel the
penalty for espionage or for aiding and abetting
the enemy is imprisonment for life.*

Coop took a lighter from his case and lit a corner of the memo. When the flame reached his fingertips, he dropped the ashes into his water glass and muttered to himself, "Dammit, Zoe, what have you gotten yourself into?"

Three

It was the copilot's turn for landing. C.T. went through the checklist, gave him a thumbs-up and sat back to observe. Even though the young man had a total of only sixteen hundred flying hours and a mere thirty-one in the Gulfstream, he greased it onto the runway like a seasoned pro. C.T. patted him on the shoulder and contacted ground control. They were directed to the executive terminal at the west end of Larnaca International.

Coop grabbed his briefcase and duffel and prepared to deplane. C.T. stepped out of the cockpit to see him off and Coop handed him a piece of paper. "Here's my international cell number. It's a little slower than going through the Agency's network, but nobody will be listening."

C.T. nodded, shoved the paper into his pocket and jotted some numbers of his own on the back of a nearby napkin. "My pager. It's on twenty-four-seven."

"Thanks, buddy. I'll see you soon."

A brand-new, chocolate brown Audi Q7 pulled up next to the Gulfstream and a man in a chauffeur's uniform got out. He looked at Coop. "Mr. Wainwright?"

"Yeah, thanks for bringing the car, but I don't need a driver. Just give me the keys and take the day off."

"I'm sorry, sir, but the car and I come together. I'm not allowed to leave it."

Coop set his briefcase on the hood of the Audi and asked the chauffer to stand beside him as he snapped it open. There was a wad of U.S. bills and a Glock 23 pistol. "This money and I come together also, but I am allowed to leave it. So, take the cash and gimme the keys."

The driver looked around. Other than Coop and himself, no one else was in sight. He dropped the keys in the case and scooped up the cash. "Enjoy this baby, it's a real road rocket. Just leave it in front of terminal when you're done with it."

When Lara had called Coop back, she told him she was staying at the Amara Hotel in Limassol. He brought it up on the Audi's GPS. It was on the Mediterranean coast, sixty-nine kilometers to the south. He hit a button on the computer and the readout switched to forty-three miles.

The GPS took Coop out of Larnaca on the B5, and a couple miles out of town he merged onto the A1. The road signs, like all others in the south of Cyprus, were written in Greek, so he relied on his GPS visual display to get him to Limassol.

About twenty miles out of Lanarca, Coop took note of a black Mercedes that had been two car lengths behind him since he left the airport. He slowed up to let the Mercedes get closer and he tilted his rearview mirror. The windshield and the side windows on the black sedan had thick black edges, indicating the presence of several layers of lead—a dead giveaway for bulletproof glass.

The GPS display switched to the diagram of a roundabout that would be coming up in three miles. Coop fell into the queue and made one revolution around the track. The Mercedes did the same. He made a second trip around the circle and so did the Mercedes. When the computer arrow pointed back to the A1, Coop floored the accelerator and the Q7 leapt onto the highway. He held the pedal down until his speedometer read 132 m.p.h. The black sedan was trying to keep up, but Coop wove in and out of traffic until the Mercedes disappeared from his rearview mirror. He took the next exit and used a local two-lane road to navigate the rest of the way to Limassol.

The Amara wasn't a run-of-the-mill tourist hotel. Nestled on a point that offered a clear 180° panoramic view of the Mediterranean, it occupied the most expensive real estate in Limassol.

Coop stepped into the lobby. It was wide open and contiguous with an infinity-edge pool that dropped off into the sea. He smiled and approached one of the front desk receptionists who was wearing the name-tag: Basil Nightingale. "Speak English?" Coop asked.

The man smirked. "Of course, sir. That is my heritage. May I be of service to you?"

"I'm here to visit a guest, Lara Graf."

"And who might you be?"

Coop's courteous smile disappeared. "I might be angry... unless you cut the snob shit. Just tell her that her friend from the U.S. is here."

The clerk's cheeks turned crimson and he stepped back. "One moment, please." He spoke into a housephone and nodded. When he returned, he had an artificial smile pasted on his face. "Ms. Graf has asked that you wait for her in the rooftop lounge."

Coop started to leave. "Sir," the clerk said.

Coop turned. "Yeah?"

The clerk's arrogance was gone. "I'd appreciate it if ya didn't report me to da manager. My name's Irv Katz and I'm really from Brooklyn, but nobody knows."

Coop smiled. "No problem, Irv. Your secret's safe with me."

Like every room in the five-star hotel, the cocktail lounge looked out over the water. Coop took a booth in the corner and ordered a Jack Daniels without ice. He was dying for a cigarette, but the three months of chemo he had gone through was enough to quell that craving.

"You made it. Thank God," a voice said.

Coop looked up. He had heard descriptions of Lara from Zoe, but he had never actually met her. She was in her middle fifties, had a soft face that Coop was sure a plastic surgeon had something to do with, and a very trim figure.

"Yeah, I made it. I've heard a lot about you from Zoe." He patted the bench seat. "Sit down and tell me everything that took place before she disappeared."

Lara slipped into the booth and put her hand on top of Coop's. "Zoe's had nothing but glowing descriptions of you. I see why."

If he didn't know what he knew, he'd guess Lara was flirting with him. It was also apparent that Lara was no stranger to this bar. The waiter placed a martini in front of her and said, "Hendriks with an olive, ma'am."

Lara slipped the toothpick between her teeth and pulled off the olive. "I am worried sick."

"Why did you guys decide to vacation in Cyprus?"

"It was Zoe's idea. I wanted to go to Australia and lie on the beach in Port Douglas...maybe do some diving off the Barrier Reef."

"But Zoe wasn't keen on Australia?"

"No, she loves Australia, but she had some business to take care of in Cyprus. It was kind of a 'kill two birds with one stone' thing, I guess."

"Business? What business? The only business she ever knew was the spy business."

Lara blotted her lipstick on a cocktail napkin and downed the martini in one swig. "I think it had something to do with those nine million dollars she took with her when she left the U.S."

"That was two years ago. Where is the money now?"

"I am not at liberty to tell you."

"Why is that?"

"I am a vice president of a Swiss bank. I cannot divulge anything about a client's finances."

"Let me rephrase the question. So, besides being your domestic partner, did Zoe also keep her money in your bank?"

"Actually, I am not really supposed to answer that question either, but I will. Yes, she deposited that money in a Swiss Commerce Bank interest-bearing savings account."

"Okay, you said on the phone that Zoe told you she was going to the lobby to talk with the concierge. How was her demeanor?"

"Exactly what do you mean by demeanor?"

"You know, was she acting differently than usual?"

Lara struck a reflective pose and appeared to be replaying the scene in her head. "She was edgy."

"Edgy. What do mean, edgy?"

"She did not want to unpack...said she would do it later. She checked her cellphone twice, then said she would be back after she talked with the concierge."

"So, you guys flew in from Zurich and drove straight from the airport to the hotel?"

Lara waved to the cocktail guy and held up her empty glass. "Well, yes, a chauffeur drove us."

"Any idea when or where Zoe was going to take care of her business?"

"No, Zoe was very private when it came to that money."

"Are you telling me as her partner and her financial advisor, you didn't know where or when Zoe would planning to make a major financial transaction?"

Lara repositioned herself on the cushion, as if a spring had just poked through. "Yes, that is what I am telling you. By the way, I have never been her financial advisor."

After thirty years in the spy business, Coop had a sixth sense for the truth. He kept staring. "Why don't I believe you?"

Lara's soft face turned hard. "Believe what you wish, but that is the way it was."

"Okay, fine, were you and Zoe having any relationship problems?"

"That, Mr. Cooper, is none of your business."

"Zoe's missing. Everything is my business."

"I thought you were here to help me find Zoe, but it looks like you are more interested in our private life."

"Lara, I'm sorry. I want the same as what you want—to find Zoe."

"Then I suggest that you start looking for her." She stomped out of the room and bumped into a confused waiter returning with her martini. She pointed back at Coop. "Give the bill to him."

The stools at the teakwood bar were filling rapidly. Coop spotted a vacant one and grabbed it. One of the two bartenders set down a cocktail napkin and a ramekin of mixed nuts and dried fruits. "Another Jack Daniels?" he asked.

"Yeah, make it neat."

Coop used his finger to rearrange the fruits so he could get to the nuts. "You ought to try one of those," a voice next to him said.

Coop turned. "Excuse me?"

An olive-skinned, good-looking guy in his early forties smiled. "Those are Cyprus figs. They dry them in the sun—a real delicacy on the island."

"You sound just like my aunt Florence, only she was a prune pusher."

"Sorry, I didn't mean to be a busybody." He thrust out his hand. "Lev Cohen."

Coop extended his hand. "Art Wainwright."

The bartender placed Coop's drink, along with the check, on the bar. Lev grabbed the chit. "Hey, I'm sorry about the unsolicited advice. Let me get this." He dropped a twenty Euro bill on the bar. "So, Art, what brings you and your wife to Cyprus?"

Coop figured Lev must have witnessed his recent confrontation with Lara. "I'm bidding on a construction project in Limassol and my wife came along for some R&R. I guess that's not working out so well."

Lev laughed. "I understand." He held up three fingers. "I'm on my third."

"You here on business or pleasure?" Coop asked.

"I'm the tour guide for a bunch of Israeli doctors that are here for what they call a seminar."

Coop nodded. He just realized it was getting late and he didn't have a place to sleep. He gulped down the remainder of his drink. "Nice talking to you, Lev. I'd better get working on my apology." He pushed away from the bar. "Thanks for the drink."

He stepped into the lobby and approached the front desk. Irv Katz wasn't there, but an attractive young lady was. "What may I do for you, sir?" she said.

"Do you have a room available tonight?"

The clerk tapped several keys on her computer. "All I have is a suite."

Coop winced. He seriously doubted he would be reimbursed for expenses on an unauthorized trip and he was about to run up a big one. "What's the rate?"

She tapped rapidly on the keys again. "Sixteen hundred euros."

Coop laughed and said, "In for a penny, in for a pound."

The clerk smiled faintly, "Sir?"

"Nothing, bad joke." Coop handed her a credit card with the name Wainwright Construction printed on the front. "I'll take it. By the way, what floor are all the doctors staying on?"

"Doctors, sir?"

"From Israel?"

"We don't have any—"

Coop waved his hand. "Mistake, my mistake. Sorry."

Four

The alarm on Coop's iPhone blared out the first stanza of the Star-Spangled Banner. He muted the sound, looked at the display—6:30 a.m.—and made a mental note to change his wake-up tune. This one made him feel like he should pop out of bed with his hand over his heart. He stepped into the bathroom and made himself comfortable on the throne before tapping in his home phone number.

Fran answered. "Coop? Is something wrong?"

"No, nothing. I know it's late there, but I just thought I should talk to you about Josh. What did he say when you told him I was heading out on an assignment?"

"He was pretty good with it. He said he understands what you do for a living, but he remembers that you were almost killed last time you went away."

"You think that depression thing will hit him again?"

"I don't think so. He got some good news at school today. He wants to tell you himself."

"Oh, that's great. I'll call tomorrow before he goes to bed."

"I'll let him know. So, how's it going over there?"

"Too early to tell, but I'm already on Zoe's girlfriend's shit list."

"Why is that?"

"She thinks I'm prying where I shouldn't pry. I'm going to talk to her after breakfast and see if I can patch things up."

"Okay, call Josh tomorrow. Love you."

"Love you too."

Coop jumped into the shower, but didn't bother with a razor. Most of the men in Cyprus were sporting at least a five-day growth; he figured he'd do the same. He slipped on a fresh pair of khakis and a lightweight polo and headed down to the restaurant near the lobby. Complimentary copies of worldwide newspapers were stacked on the maître d's table. Coop picked up a copy of the *Times* and took a seat in the open-air restaurant at a table made of tiles arranged in a typical Mediterranean-mosaic. He ordered sweet coffee and a Halloumi-Mint Scone. Although he wasn't quite sure what that was, he remembered the sun-dried figs in the bar were pretty good, so he figured he couldn't go too far wrong ordering a local pastry.

He skimmed through the paper while waiting for his breakfast to arrive. The scone was the familiar English style, but with a unique bitter Cypriot flavor. On the other hand, the coffee was different from any other he had tasted. It was served in a demitasse, was very strong—kind of a mixture of Turkish and Greek—and alongside was served a glass of cold water. He noticed other people sipping the dark brown mixture very slowly, so he followed suit. When he came to the bottom of the cup, he realized why such care was being taken. Pasted to the bottom was a layer of brown sludge. He gulped down the cold water and didn't ask for a refill on the coffee.

He went back to skimming his newspaper until an article buried on the bottom of page six caught his eye. The headline read: *Israel sentences three Iranian spies to life in prison.* "They're not messing around," he muttered.

Coop signed his room number on the check and approached the front desk. Basil was back on duty. "A top of the morning to you, sir," he said.

"Hey, Irv, cut the shit, it's me. Remember?"

The Brooklyn native smiled. "Oh, yeah, how ya doin', Mr. Wainwright?"

"I'm doing great. Would you ring Lara Graf's room? Tell her I'm in the lobby."

"No can do."

Coop's eyes narrowed. "And why is that, Irv?"

"Because she checked out about an hour and a half ago."

Coop hid his astonishment, turned away from the reception desk and found himself face to face with Lev Cohen. "Good morning, Mr. Wainwright, or should I say Mr. Cooper." The Israeli pointed to a set of chairs on the patio. "May we talk?"

They settled into a couple of plush cushions set on wicker frames and Lev took out a pack of Dunhills. He tapped a cigarette out the top and held it in Coop's direction.

Coop waved him off. "You go ahead. I smoked my last one two years ago."

Lev lit the cigarette, took a deep drag of the blended English tobacco and let it out through his nostrils. "I understand. I'm going to quit soon myself."

Coop knew that phrase well. He had uttered it dozens of times before getting lung cancer. "So, you know my name," he said.

"I do."

"Then you know my profession."

"Intimately. And you know I'm not a tour guide."

"I do."

"Then you know my profession."

Coop grinned. "Intimately. You're a Mossad agent."

Lev grinned back. "I assume you've come to Cyprus looking for your former partner, Zoe Fields."

The sound of Zoe's name signaled the end of the fun and games and the smile disappeared from Coop's face. "Why would Mossad care about that?"

"Because we're looking for her also."

"Why?"

"Because we think Zoe Fields is either an agent or a sympathizer of Iran."

Coop's jaw dropped. "That's absurd."

"Is it?"

"Yeah, it is."

"Two years ago, you and Ms. Fields worked a case in Iraq and ended up with nine million dollars of Iran's money."

"It wasn't Iran's money. They paid it out for the delivery of a load of contraband."

"Contraband that you and Ms. Fields destroyed and money that ended up in a Zurich bank account belonging to Zoe Fields."

"Okay, enough of this shit. That's none of Israel's business."

Lev snuffed out his cigarette. "Well, we think it is."

Five

Coop tapped a ten-digit number into his cell, let it ring and hung up. Two minutes later his phone buzzed. "Is that you, C.T.?"

"Yeah, what's up?"

"File a flight plan to Tel Aviv. I'll meet you at the plane in an hour."

Coop tipped the attendant five Euros and threw his bags into the back seat of the Audi. He checked the GPS for the nearest roundabout leading to the A1, then peeled rubber and headed for it. As soon as he was on the highway, he accelerated, keeping it just under a hundred as he headed back to Larnaca. When he checked his rearview mirror, that pesty black Mercedes was on his tail again.

He knew he could outrun it, but he was tired of being hounded. He slammed on the brakes and slid to a stop on the dirt shoulder of the pavement. The Mercedes driver was taken by surprise and had to pass Coop before skidding onto the shoulder in front of him. Coop opened his briefcase, withdrew his Glock and released the safety. He tucked it under his belt.

He put the transmission into neutral and ran up the RPMs by pumping on the accelerator until they reached 6500—the bottom of the redline. He held his foot steady and as he suspected, the driver's door of the Mercedes opened; he jammed the transmission into low gear, popped the clutch and floored the gas pedal. With the RPMs already near max, the Audi leapt forward like a wild animal just let out of a cage. Coop put a mental bullseye on the open door and sent it flying skyward when his front end rammed it at 68 mph.

Coop slammed on his brakes and screeched to a stop. He withdrew his Glock and jumped from his car at the same time as a man exited the Mercedes through the portal where the door used to be. Coop raised his pistol and gripped it with both hands.

The man raised his arms and smiled broadly. "Hey, Cooper, take it easy. It's me, Lev."

Coop kept his pistol raised and inched toward the Mercedes. He peered inside. It was empty. "Goddammit, Cohen, what the fuck do you think you're doing?"

"May I lower my hands?"

Coop tucked the Glock back into his belt. "I don't give a damn what you do."

Lev shoved a Dunhill between his lips and lit it. "I didn't take you for a guy who would overreact this way."

"Overreact? What would you do if a bulletproof car was following you around?"

Lev let the smoke drift out from the corners of his lips. "Yeah, I guess I would've done the same. I just wanted to see where you were headed."

"Well, next time try asking. I'm headed to Tel Aviv to talk to your director."

"Oh, that's perfect. Can I bum a ride?"

Coop looked at Lev like he was just beamed down from Nimbus III. "Man, you've got gall."

"In my country it's called chutzpah. So, you got room?"

Coop looked at his Audi Q7. Steam was billowing out from under the hood; the cooling system was obviously trashed. He retrieved his briefcase and his duffel and threw them in the back seat of the Mercedes. "Let's go," he said.

C.T. was waiting on the tarmac next to the Gulfstream when the doorless Mercedes pulled to a stop ten feet away. Coop got out and waved. C.T. looked at the car and then at Coop. "Some people just rent convertibles. Where's the Audi?" he said.

"I had a little car trouble. Give them a call and have them pick it up on the A1 just north of Limassol...oh, and have them bill any damages to Wainwright Construction."

Lev Cohen strolled a three-sixty around the private jet and paused next to Coop. "Man, you guys travel in comfort. I get economy class on El Al."

"Grab your bag and get in," Coop said.

Lev handed his carry-on to the flight attendant and took a seat facing Coop. "Do you need a place to stay in Tel Aviv?" he asked.

Coop hadn't given it much thought. Normally he would stay in the Agency's apartment not far from the embassy, but this mission was covert—even to the director. "Yeah, what do you suggest?"

"I've got a two-bedroom on the beach. Stay as long as you want, but bring your own booze."

"What will your third wife have to say about that?" Coop said. Lev laughed and Coop joined him. "You've never been married, have you?"

Lev shook his head. "So, you want to bunk at my place or not?"

Coop thought about it. "You want to pick my brain to find Zoe Fields, don't you?"

The smile dropped from Lev's face and his dark brown eyes turned to steel. "Look, Coop, I don't have anything against your friend. If she has no ties to Iran, then she has nothing to fear from me. Let's work together and find her."

"I'll let you know. Does my room have a private bath?"

Six

The cab dropped them off in front of a condominium complex on Frischmann Beach—part of Israel's Mediterranean coastline. They were only two blocks from the U.S. embassy, but were in an upscale resort area with high-rise hotels lining the boulevard. Lev paid the driver and motioned Coop to follow him. They took the elevator to the eighth floor where Lev opened the door to a luxurious condo. "Not bad for a government employee," Coop said.

"Your room is down the hall."

The accommodations were a lot better than Coop's hotel suite. He still had a view of the Mediterranean and it wasn't costing him sixteen-hundred Euros a night. He ran through a shower, changed clothes and joined his host in the living room. Lev handed him a double old-fashioned. "Jack Daniels neat," he said.

"I thought the booze wasn't included."

Lev grinned. "I was only kidding." He took a pull off a bottle of Goldstar beer. "So, are we going to help each other?"

"Do you trust me?"

"No, do you trust me?"

"No. So, I guess we get started," Coop said.

Lev opened up a map of the Middle East and pointed to the island of Cyprus. "This is where Zoe was last seen." He moved his finger down the map. "Tel Aviv is here, two hundred miles south." He gave a broad-brush stroke across the right side of the map. "From Cyprus, it's a hundred and twenty-five miles to Beirut—two-fifteen to Damascus."

Coop looked at the map. "How far to Iran? If you're so sure Zoe works for them, wouldn't she go there?"

"It's a thousand miles east. I checked all the scheduled flights and private planes that left Cyprus yesterday. No good-looking blondes fitting her description flew off the island, so she must have left by boat. Odds are, she travelled to Beirut. It's the shortest trip."

Coop thought about Lev's theory. "Okay, I'll call C.T. He can have the Gulfstream ready to go first thing in the morning,"

"Sounds good," Lev said. "But I'm going to have to travel under a U.S. passport. Lebanon is not exactly our best friend and my name is on their 'most wanted' list."

"Okay, do you need one?"

Lev moved to his desk and opened the bottom drawer. He took out a dozen passports and thumbed through them before making his choice. "No problem, I have one...Richard Hughes from Wichita."

"What about visas?" Coop asked.

"Yeah, we'll need those to get into Lebanon. Can your embassy deliver for us?"

"I can see what they can do, but I need you to get me a meeting with your director. I still have to find out why Zoe's in his bullseye."

"No problem. There's a big reception at Beit Aghion, the prime minister's residence, tomorrow night and the director will be there. I'll set it up for you."

Lev gave Coop directions to the U.S. embassy. Although it was only a couple blocks away, just on the edge of the resort district, Coop didn't think it would look good for a deputy director to arrive on foot. He hailed a cab. The driver wrinkled his nose at the two-block fare, but got over it when Coop handed him a U.S. twenty-dollar bill and told him to keep the change.

Two parade-dressed Marines were doing guard duty from a kiosk in front of the fenced embassy building. The one with the extra stripe on his sleeve stepped out. "May I help you, sir?"

Coop left Art Wainwright in his wallet and instead handed over his badge and his agency credentials. "I need to see the ambassador. It's important."

The Marine stepped back into the kiosk and picked up a phone. He nodded several times before returning to where Coop was waiting, then handed back his credentials and signaled for the gate to open. "Third floor...the ambassador will be waiting. Good day, sir."

Coop was escorted into the ambassador's office and did a double take. "Billings? Jim Billings?" he said.

The ambassador was all smiles. "How're you doing, Coop?"

"When did you leave Baghdad?"

"Not long after you did, but the M.P.s weren't chasing me." Billings pointed to a tea pot. "How about a cup of Darjeeling Black Leaf?"

Coop had been through this drill before with Jim Billings. The ambassador had a fetish for exotic teas, but Coop couldn't stand the stuff. "Got any coffee?" Coop asked.

Billings wrinkled his nose and poured from another pot as if the contents were laced with arsenic. "You never had any refinement, Agent Cooper."

Coop took a sip. "It's Deputy Director Cooper now."

Billings squeezed a lemon into his cup. "Oh, yes, I heard. How's that working out?"

"Fine. Listen Jim, I need a favor."

"Why would I do you a favor after the way you barged into my apartment and threatened my mistress and me?"

"Why? Because I could have told your wife and ruined your marriage, but I didn't. That's why."

Billings clasped his hands together and began twiddling his thumbs. He bit his lip and replayed that ugly scene from Baghdad. "Okay, I owe you one. What's the favor?"

"I need two visas into Lebanon. One for myself and one for an Israeli agent traveling under a U.S. passport."

"When?"

"By tomorrow morning."

"Impossible."

Coop drained his coffee cup and stood to leave. "You know, Jim, it's never too late to leak a juicy story." He dropped the two passports on Billings' desk. "I'll pick the visas up at eight tomorrow morning."

Seven

Coop rolled out of bed and looked out the window where the sun was beginning to rise over the water. He checked his phone; it was 6:45. He threw on the same clothes he had worn the day before and joined Lev in the kitchen. He was busy adding ingredients to a frying pan. "Coffee is on the counter," Lev said.

Coop poured himself a cup and inhaled the aroma coming from the stove. "Man, that smells good."

Lev smiled as he smashed up tomatoes in the pan and added a few chopped bell peppers. "You ever have garlic for breakfast?"

"Not that I remember."

Lev dumped in a chopped spoonful. "You will now." He stirred the mixture and sprinkled in a few garbanzos along with some sort of white cheese. When his masterpiece began to thicken, he used a spoon to make a couple of wells and dropped two eggs into each. He covered the pan and poured himself a cup of coffee. "So, how did you sleep?"

"Like a baby. You've got a beautiful place here."

"Thanks. I like it."

"I noticed you have a Hamilton safe in the closet of the bedroom I'm using. It's American made. I have one almost like it."

"Yeah, almost all the good stuff comes from the States."

"Is yours a digital or a wheel opener?" Coop asked.

"Neither." He held up his thumb. "It works off the print of this guy. Hey, did you get the visas?"

"We'll pick them up on the way to the airport."

Lev nodded. "We'll have to be back by nine tonight if you want to meet the Mossad director."

"Shouldn't be a problem. It's only a thirty-minute flight."

"Unless we get detained." Lev said. "Then it could be a thirty-year sentence." He turned off the burner and dished out his culinary creation. He handed a plate to Coop. "Shakshuka. Every country in this part of the world claims it as their own."

They called a cab to take them to the airport, but first they made a stop in front of the embassy. Coop stepped up to the kiosk and showed his credentials. "You have something for me? Deputy Director Cooper?" The marine handed Coop an envelope. He looked inside, approved of the contents and got back into the taxi.

The engines of the Gulfstream were already purring at idle when the cab dropped Coop and Lev on the tarmac. They hustled aboard and within ten minutes were airborne. As soon as they leveled off, C.T. joined them in the passenger compartment. "I'll need those visas to get a landing clearance," he said.

Coop dug through his briefcase and handed them to him. "If you get hassled, we'll scrub the mission."

C.T. smiled. "Don't worry, I've been through this drill before."

Beirut-Rafic Hariri International wasn't used to handling planes registered in the U.S. As soon as C.T. cut the engines, two men dressed in double-breasted black suits boarded the plane. "Who is in charge here?" the taller of the two asked. Coop stepped forward and raised his index finger. "Why are you here?" the guy said.

Coop handed the man their passports, visas and a business card identifying himself as the president of Wainwright Construction. "I'm Art Wainwright." He pointed to Lev. "This is my V.P. Richard Hughes. We're bidding a job for a new Hilton here in Beirut."

The man scrutinized the documents with a smug smirk across his face. "Why would Lebanon need another Western hotel?"

Coop shrugged. "I don't know. Better ask your minister of commerce. Hey, we've flown five thousand miles and we're only scheduled to be here for two hours. Are we good to go?"

The man pointed to his partner. "Agent Khalil will accompany you." He handed back the credentials and stomped out of the plane.

Coop asked the flight attendant to offer Khalil something to drink and Coop stepped into the cockpit. "Hey, C.T., what kind of car did you arrange for?"

"The usual, a Mercedes. Why?"

"Cancel it and get the smallest two-door you can. Hey, how tall are you?"

"Six-three."

"What d'ya weigh?"

"Two-thirty."

"Perfect, plan to join us when the car gets here."

Coop went back to tell Lev and Khalil the car was late, but it would be here in a few minutes. When it arrived, Coop was ecstatic. It was a two-door, Toyota compact. "Okay, everyone, let's get going," he said.

Coop directed Khalil, Lev and C.T. to share the tiny back seat— he sat up front with the driver. As soon as they left the airport, Coop checked the temperature gauges. Inside the car the temperature was a comfortable sixty-eight degrees Fahrenheit; outside it was hovering around ninety-three. He leaned over and turned off the air-conditioning switch.

In order to prolong the ride, Coop asked the driver for a tour of the downtown district. Beirut was once called the Paris of the

Middle East. It still possessed much of that charm, its cafe culture, chic fashion, and French influence, but intermingled along with the sidewalk cafés and local shops were bombed-out or burned-out buildings—courtesy of the local terrorists.

The air inside the Toyota quickly ripened and everyone began to sweat, especially Khalil, who had on a suit and was wedged between the two biggest guys in the car. When he couldn't take any more of it, he leaned forward and said, "Mister Wainwright, have the driver stop and let me out for a cold drink." Coop did as he was told and Khalil hustled inside a local convenience store.

As soon as he was out of sight, Coop said to the driver, "Let's go, we'll come back for him later."

Lev took over and directed the driver to the waterfront. He and Coop stepped out and Coop instructed the driver to take C.T. back to the airport. The driver acknowledged and the Toyota sped off. "Who's your contact?" Coop said.

"I've got a local guy who's used to working both sides of the street. He has a boat shop two blocks from here."

Coop was amazed that Lev could even find the place. The waterfront was lined with unmarked doors and signs written in Arabic. Wedged between a fishing supply shop and a falafel restaurant, Lev spotted a dilapidated wooden door. He banged on it.

A guy with skin that was suntanned to the point of wrinkles, dressed in a grimy white robe, opened the door. He immediately recognized Lev and hustled the two men inside; then he peered up and down the street to make sure there were no followers. When he was satisfied they were alone, he closed the door. He spoke in broken English. "Something to drink? Some Arak, maybe?"

"No. Thank you, though," Lev said. "Listen, Mahir, we have to know if an American woman entered Lebanon from Cyprus on a boat within the last forty-eight hours."

"My friend, I am a good informant, not a good magician."

Coop slipped a handwritten piece of paper from his pocket. On it was a list of names and countries: Zoe Fields, USA, Frieda Warner, Germany, Anna Tavros, Cyprus, Olivia Lee, Singapore. He handed it to Lev. "She would have been travelling under one of these passports."

Lev took out a wad of Euros and set it on the table. "Let's see some magic."

Mahir began tapping numbers into his cell phone and jabbering in Arabic. Forty-five minutes later he turned to Lev. "I cannot...how do you say it...guarantee...to you that she did not come in on a small private boat or fishing scow, but she did not get to Beirut on a ferry or a charter. My people...they checked those records."

Lev signaled Mahir to pick up the money. "How easy would it be to make the trip from Cyprus to Beirut in a small boat?" Lev asked.

Mahir raised his brows and rolled his eyes. "Even the fishermen...they vomit."

The high-low pulsating sound of a police siren echoed from the street. It got louder and louder until it appeared to be directly in front of the shop. Mahir pushed against a wall that opened into a back room. He motioned for Coop and Lev to step inside and then he pulled the partition back in place.

Before Mahir could unbolt the front door, a battering ram imploded it into the room and Khalil, accompanied by three uniformed policemen, forced their way inside. Khalil immediately began interrogating Mahir in Arabic.

Lev whispered to Coop, "He wants to know where we are."

Khalil began yelling and the nauseating sound of knuckles striking bone echoed from the adjacent room. The two agents could hear Mahir moaning and it was clear to Coop that, with the beating he was taking, it wouldn't be long before Mahir caved. "We have to get outta here," Coop said.

"I can't just leave Mahir. Maybe—"

"Maybe, what? As soon as they break him, we're all dead men." Coop surveyed the room. It was being used for the storage of boat parts, and boxes were piled to the ceiling, but a faint sliver of light was sneaking through between a couple of the cartons. "Gimme a hand," he said.

Coop stood on a chair and passed boxes down to Lev. A small window covered in grime appeared from behind the crates. Coop twisted the latch and pushed against it, but it was rusted shut and wouldn't budge. He looked around the room several times until he spotted a boat anchor leaning against the far wall. He pointed to it. "Hey, hand that thing up to me."

Lev did as he was told. Coop used the tip of the anchor like an axe and chopped the glass out of the frame. "Let's go," he said and scrambled head first through the opening.

Lev hesitated for a moment until he heard a single gunshot come from the other room. He jumped onto the chair, scrambled to the top of the boxes and started through the broken-out window. His had hesitated too long. One of the uniforms crashed through the fake wall and fired a shot that caught Lev in the left leg.

From the outside, Coop watched Lev as he crawled through the window. When he heard the shot, he saw Lev wince. He reached up and grabbed Lev by the shoulders and pulled him into the alley. The bottom left side of his khakis was covered in blood. Coop pulled off his belt, wrapped it around the bloodstain and cinched it tight; the bleeding stopped. "Can you walk?" Coop asked.

Lev took a step, but his leg wouldn't support the weight and he fell to the ground. Coop raised him up and slung Lev's arm over his shoulder. Coop trudged up the alley lugging Lev along with him, but they weren't making very good time. Coop knew it wouldn't be long before their pursuers would be on top of them. He spotted an open door about ten yards ahead and peered inside. It led to the back room of a kitchen where he could see two men up front feverishly cooking falafels. He pulled Lev inside, closed the door and slid the dead bolt.

A minute later he heard Khalil yelling at the policemen. Voices came from right outside the door and someone tried to turn the knob, but when the door wouldn't open, the Arabic chatter faded as the posse took off up the alley.

Coop laid Lev down, loosened the belt from the bloodstain and ripped his pantleg up the side. There was both an entry and an exit wound—a good sign the bullet had passed through without catching any bones. He tore a nearby dish towel in half and wrapped it tightly around the punctures. "How're you doing?"

Lev forced a smile. "I've done better."

Out of the corner of his eye, Coop spotted one of the cooks heading in their direction. The guy hustled into the back room, picked up a can of cooking oil and froze in his tracks. Next to a sack of garbanzos he spied Coop and Lev lying on the floor; he began to jabber in Arabic. Coop looked at Lev. "What's he saying?"

"He says he's going to call the police."

Coop stood and held up his hands. "No, no, don't do that." He turned to Lev. "Give me whatever money you have with you."

"Pocket...left pocket."

Coop reached in and pulled out nine one-hundred-euro bills. He held them up for the wide-eyed cook to see. Coop could sense the man was weighing his options. He shoved the cash into the guy's hand. The man hesitated, then smiled and grasped the money. He took the can of oil with him and went back to the kitchen.

Coop opened his cell, dialed a set of numbers and hung up. In thirty seconds, his phone buzzed. "C.T., is that you?" Coop said.

"Yeah, what's happening?"

"I need you to get a car and pick us up."

"Where are you?"

"I'm not sure, but I'll have Lev text an address. Call me when you're out front."

"Okay, give me an hour."

"Make it thirty minutes or it might be too late."

"Gotcha."

"And C.T....have your copilot file a flight plan and have the turbines turning and ready to go."

Sweat was dripping down Lev's forehead and he blinked a couple times to clear it from his eyes. Coop held the cell phone up next to him and Lev managed to tap in the address in spite of a trembling finger. "Good job." Coop said. He laid Lev's head on his lap and wiped his forehead with what was left of the towel. "Hang in there, buddy, the cavalry is on its way."

Twenty minutes later the cell phone buzzed. "C.T.?"

"I'm out front."

"Okay, do you see an alley nearby?"

"Yeah, if you could call it that."

"We're about ten yards into it."

Coop couldn't get Lev to his feet, so he put his arms under Lev's armpits and dragged him toward the back door. He slid the dead bolt and forced it open. C.T. spotted them and jumped from the passenger side of a Mercedes sedan to help get Lev into the back seat. As soon as the doors were slammed shut, the driver floored the gas pedal and took off up the alley. "I'll have you at the airport in fifteen minutes," he said.

Coop's head popped up. "You're American?"

"Don't tell the Lebanese government. They think I'm a Canadian running a two-bit limo business. I was supposed to be your driver today, but your pilot said you wanted a smaller car."

"Are you an Agency guy?"

The driver laughed. "No, just an ex-pat trying to make a living off a little espionage." He dropped them beside the door of the Gulfstream and the copilot had the plane in the air in less than five minutes.

Eight

C.T. radioed ahead for an ambulance and it was on the tarmac when they landed. By the time they reached the emergency room, the E.M.T.s had Lev floating on morphine and he was giggling at their corny jokes. The E.R. doc upped his dose, cleansed the wounds and sent him off to surgery.

Coop hung around the waiting room until almost six p.m. before he entered the 3rd floor post-op room where Lev was half awake. "How're you doing, buddy?"

Lev's eyes tried to open, but they wouldn't go past halfway. "I'm fine...doc says...he says...says he sewed up the muscle." He drifted off.

Coop gently shook Lev's shoulder and his lids made an attempt to open. "Hey, Lev, I have to know how I'll get into that reception tonight...you know...at the P.M.'s residence."

"Oh, yeah...get me my phone."

Coop spotted it on the table with Lev's other personal items and tried to hand it to him. "I'm too gr...groggy to dial. Push the number for Rachel," Lev said.

Coop followed instructions and held the phone up to Lev's ear. "Rachel, it's me. I got...got myself shot." He closed his eyes and opened them again. "No, I'm in the hospital, but I'm fine. Listen, pick up a guy named Cooper at my place around eight o'clock and get him into the reception tonight...and make sure he gets to talk... to talk to the director."

Coop traded Lev's phone for the key to his condo. "Thanks, buddy. See ya tomorrow."

Coop figured he was due for a little luck and it came in the form of dress wear. He and Lev were both six-two and very close to the same waist size. Lev's tux fitted him perfectly. Around a quarter to eight there was knock on the door. Coop found himself looking at a beautiful, dark-haired, brown-eyed woman wrapped in a chic cocktail dress. "Mr. Cooper?"

"Call me Coop. I'm guessing you're Rachel."

"Wow, Lev didn't tell me I was picking up a rocket scientist." Coop wasn't sure if he should laugh or be insulted. "Just a joke," she said. He hesitated and then broke out laughing.

Rachel's limo driver connected with the highway going southeast, away from the water. "How long to Jerusalem?" Coop asked.

"About forty-five minutes." Rachel opened a cabinet. "Drink?"

Coop looked inside. There was a bottle of Jack Daniels. He narrowed his eyes. "I'm guessing Lev told you about me way before he called you from the hospital."

"We're all in the same business, Coop. You know that."

Coop sighed. "Okay, Jack, no ice." She opened a bottle and poured a generous amount into a glass. He took a sip. "Listen, Rachel, what language will be spoken tonight?"

"Don't worry. A few people will be speaking Hebrew, but English is the universal language of choice."

The driver entered an upscale Jerusalem neighborhood and pulled to a stop at the corner of Smolenskin and Balfour. What looked like a full platoon of soldiers dressed in combat gear was stationed around the perimeter of the old estate. Two of the guards approached the limo. Rachel showed them their credentials and had a brief conversation in Hebrew. The limo was waved through the gates.

Once inside the mansion, Coop felt like he was at a wedding reception in the Hamptons. A small orchestra was playing classical music and uniformed cocktail waitresses were passing hors d'oeuvres and taking drink orders. He declined on both.

Rachel excused herself and disappeared into another room. Ten minutes later she was back. "Director Mizrahi is waiting in the study." She pointed to a set of double doors.

Coop wasn't sure of the protocol in this setting, but it didn't seem appropriate to knock, so he turned the knob and walked right in. A man in his early sixties with thinning hair and wearing wire framed glasses turned to greet him with a thrust-out hand. "Abraham Mizrahi. I've been looking forward to your visit, Deputy Director Cooper."

"Really? For how long?"

"Since the day Zoe Fields disappeared from Cyprus." Mizrahi removed a cigar from a humidor and offered one to Coop.

Coop shook his head. "No thanks, but you go ahead. So, you knew I'd be coming."

"We spies are a predictable lot, are we not?" The director settled into a leather armchair and motioned Coop to do the same.

"So, this meeting was planned even before I ran into Lev Cohen?" Coop said.

Mizrahi snipped the end from the cigar and licked the outside paper before lighting it with a stick match. He inhaled deeply and let the smoke out slowly through pursed lips. "Lev Cohen was merely the conduit to get you here."

"Okay, how about we stop playing games and you tell me what's really going on."

Mizrahi tapped the tip of his cigar on a glass ashtray. "Your ex-partner appears to be either an Iranian sympathizer or an agent of Iran and we want you to help us find her."

"That's bullshit and even if it weren't, I wouldn't help you."

Mizrahi curled his lips and let out a smoke ring. "I know you want to think that, but I have evidence to the contrary."

"Let's see it."

Mizrahi picked up a house phone. "Please send in some food, a brandy and...." He looked at Coop.

"Jack Daniels, no ice."

The director finished his order, hung up the phone and stepped to his desk. He opened the top drawer and took out a document. "What does this look like to you?" He handed Coop the paper.

Coop read it from top to bottom. "It looks like a receipt for nine million dollars."

"And who wired the money?"

"Zoe Fields."

"And who received that money?"

Coop ran his finger down the printed lines. "Looks like some agency in Tehran."

A smug expression took over Mizrahi's face. "The last time I checked, Tehran was the capital of Iran."

Coop tossed the paper back to him. "You've been in this business long enough to know that things aren't always as they seem."

"That is true, Mr. Cooper, but these things don't seem very good. Your friend Ms. Fields agreed to send that money to me here in Israel, but instead she sent it to Iran."

Coop didn't answer; he just sat and watched Mizrahi blow smoke rings. A knock came from the door. "Bring it in," the director said in a loud voice. The door opened and a woman with long frizzy black hair and overdone makeup entered pushing a cart full of food and drinks. She turned her back to Coop as she transferred the plates and glasses to a coffee table.

Mizrahi rested his cigar in the ashtray. "Thank you, miss ...?"

"Shira. Shira Reuben, sir."

"Thank you, Shira."

The woman turned to leave. She was face to face with Coop and eye contact was unavoidable. Even with the disguise, he'd know those eyes anywhere.

Nine

Zoe's gaze lingered for a moment before turning back toward the director. "Will there be anything else?" she asked.

"No, Shira. Thank you very much." Zoe pushed the tea cart toward the door and left.

Coop stood. "I'll think about what you said."

"That's it? You will think about it?"

Coop took one last sip from his glass and set it on the table. "Thanks for the drink. Like I said, I'll think about it."

Coop left the study and entered the main parlor where the party was going stronger than ever. The men in their tuxedos and women in their cocktail dresses were eating more, drinking heavier and laughing louder while servers passed the food and drinks among them.

It took twenty minutes of chasing waitresses around before Coop was convinced that Zoe wasn't in the room. He noticed a swinging door being used by the servers to go in and out of the salon. He pushed it open and stepped into a large kitchen. A dozen chefs were busy creating hors d'oeuvres and setting them on the servers' empty trays.

Coop approached the chef who was giving the orders. "Excuse me, do you speak English?"

The man appeared annoyed with Coop for invading his space. "Yes, do you need something, sir? I am very busy."

"Yeah, sorry. I'm looking for Shira Reuben."

The chef tilted his head toward a corner where a uniformed waitress had her back to them. Coop approached the woman and tapped her shoulder. "Zoe?" The woman turned. She was in her middle sixties and had more than her share of age spots dotting her face. "Oh, I'm sorry," Coop said. "I was looking for Shira Reuben."

"I am Shira Reuben."

Coop apologized and stepped back into the main salon. Rachel spotted him and wove her way through the crowd to join him. "I trust your meeting with the director went well."

Coop gazed around the room as he answered. "Yeah, it went fine."

"Why don't you take a stroll of the grounds, they're beautiful. We'll plan to leave in about an hour."

Coop welcomed the chance to search a little longer for Zoe. "Yeah, maybe I'll take a look at them," he said. It took a good forty-five minutes to check the face of every female server on the property; Zoe was not among them. He went back inside the residence and rejoined Rachel, who was waiting in the same spot he had left her. "I'm ready, let's go," he said.

Rachel made a cell call and dropped the phone back into her purse. "The limo will meet us at the front gate."

As soon as they were settled in the rear seats, the driver headed west and joined the highway back to Tel Aviv. Coop checked the time; it was a quarter to twelve in Israel, but only a quarter to five back in D.C. He tapped in his home phone number.

The phone was picked up on the first ring. "Dad? Is that you?"

"Yeah, Josh, it's me. How're you doing?"

"I'm great. Is everything going okay with your assignment?"

"Yeah, it's fine. Listen, I want to apologize for leaving before I got a chance to talk to you. I know I promised you I'd never do this again, but..."

Josh interrupted. "Dad, it's okay. I'm almost fourteen. I understand."

"You sure?"

"Yes. Mom explained it to me and told me how Aunt Zoe needs your help. I understand. I do."

Coop wanted a cigarette so bad and there was a box of them in the console of the limo, but he fought off the urge. "You sure?"

"I'm sure."

"Hey, your mom said there was some good news you had for me."

The inflection of Josh's voice sounded like he was smiling. "I made the freshman basketball team."

"Oh, Josh, that's great. How big is the roster?"

"Fifteen, but only twelve guys get to dress for the games."

This was always Josh's dream and Coop's gut tightened at the thought that Josh might not make the final twelve. "When's the first game?"

"Two weeks from Friday. Can you make it home by then?"

Coop had been down this road before—making promises he didn't know if he could keep. "I'll be there. I promise."

"Oh, that's so great, Dad. I miss you."

"I miss you too. I'll see you in a couple weeks. Hey, put Mom on."

Coop could hear Josh yelling into the kitchen for Fran to pick up. A couple of seconds later, she did. "Coop? How's it going over there?"

Coop turned away from Rachel for some privacy. "Right now, it's a shit storm, but hopefully it'll get better."

"I couldn't help but hear part of your conversation with Josh. Can you really be back for his game?"

"I'm going to try."

"He's counting on it, Coop. Try really hard."

Coop dropped the phone into his pocket. "Are you married?" he asked Rachel.

"No, I tried it once, but this job isn't very conducive to maintaining a relationship. How do you manage it?"

"I'm not sure. I don't think I manage it very well."

Ten

It was almost two a.m. by the time Coop got back to Lev's condo. He was pretty wired. He poured himself a brandy, settled into Lev's La-Z-Boy recliner and turned the TV to CNN's English-speaking channel. The newscaster was abruptly interrupted by an announcement. *Breaking news from Jerusalem. Abraham Mizrahi, director of Israel's Mossad, was assassinated in the prime minister's residence during a social event this evening. We will provide more information as it comes in.*

Coop grabbed his phone from the table and punched in a few numbers. A minute later it buzzed. "C.T.?"

"Yeah, what's up?"

"Get your crew together and fly the plane out of Israel ASAP. Like fifteen minutes from now."

"Okay, are you coming?"

"No, go back to Cyprus and wait for my call. If you don't hear from me in a week, head back to D.C."

C.T. knew better than to ask for an explanation. "Will do," he said. "And good luck."

Coop rushed into the bedroom, stuffed his clothes into his duffel, grabbed his briefcase and left by the back staircase. Once on the boulevard, he headed in the direction of the hotels. He suddenly realized he was still wearing Lev's tux. He ducked into an alley and exchanged it for a pair of khakis, a sweatshirt and a baseball cap. He dropped Lev's formal wear into a dumpster.

Unlike the United States, where bars close at two a.m., Israel's drinking scene doesn't even get going until that hour. Coop slipped into a booth near the back of the Carlton Hotel's sports lounge. He ordered a Perrier and pretended to be watching the replay of a soccer game on the big screen TV. The sound was muted, so he didn't know what was being said, but when the match was preempted for a news flash, he had no trouble recognizing a 60-inch photo of himself along with the English caption: *Suspect sought.*

By six a.m., the bar was nearly empty and Coop knew he would have to move on, but he was running out of options. All his phony passports were in the plane, so he was stuck with his own authentic one. He couldn't use his personal credit card, but he figured he could use the one for Wainwright Construction—or could he? Lev knew this was his alias and it wouldn't take long for Mossad to track him. He did have twenty-thousand U.S. dollars in cash that he kept in a concealed compartment of his briefcase.

Coop hadn't shaved since he arrived in Cyprus, so his scruffy beard was beginning to camouflage his facial features. He bought a pair of cheap sunglasses from a street vendor to cover his eyes and with the baseball cap pulled low, it was unlikely anyone would match him to the photos appearing on TV or in the newspapers. He tossed his cell phone off a pier into the Mediterranean.

He took a cab to the train station and bought a ticket out of Tel Aviv. In an hour and twenty minutes he stepped into Jerusalem's Yitzhak Navon Station. He went into a store that sold an assortment of souvenirs and bought a burner phone that was programmed for ten hours of use.

Over the years, Coop and Zoe had worked at least a dozen foreign operations together. They had a plan in place if ever they became separated. Coop would put a coded ad in the personals section of the nearest English-language newspaper. It was a longshot, but it was all he had. He placed it in the *Jerusalem Post*.

Coop found a bed in a hostel for sixty-two shekels a night. He did the math and realized that was only about twenty bucks, so he paid for three nights in advance. It was Friday and Coop was expecting to see his ad in print the next day, but he had forgotten that in Israel the sabbath was celebrated on Saturday and therefore, the *Post* wouldn't come out until Sunday morning. He used the time to take a tour bus around the city and scope it out.

Early Sunday morning, Coop walked to the Yehuda market, where he picked up a copy of the *Post* and a cup of Roasters Coffee. He found his ad on the bottom of page twenty-four: **Wanted, a partner for adventure. Text: 972-558-6981-42.**

He hadn't finished his first cup before his phone began to vibrate. He was amazed how many adventure addicts resided in Jerusalem. They ran the gamut from sexual explorers to mountain climbers. By ten a.m. he had deleted thirty-six messages. The thirty-seventh was the one he had been hoping for: **If you'd like a view of the Potomac, contact me.**

Coop texted back: **The Wailing Wall in one hour.**

Eleven

On the way to the old city, Coop bought a prayer book, an inexpensive prayer shawl and a kippah to cover his head. When he arrived at the wall, he joined a large group of men who were reciting Hebrew passages from frayed prayer books.

The women were segregated about twenty yards away. Coop kept his head tilted toward the prayer book, but his eyes were on the women. Although they covered themselves in shawls, he could tell by their posture and their gaits that most were quite old.

He stole a peek at his phone; it was eleven-forty-eight. His hookup was almost an hour late. He waited another thirty minutes before turning to leave. When he did, he bumped smack into a mourner and knocked him on his butt. "Oh, pardon me...please... I'm so sorry."

He bent down to help the slightly framed man to his feet. The guy raised his head and said, "How's the view of the Potomac?"

Coop did a double take. "Zoe?"

"Hey, boss, can you help an old man to his feet?"

Zoe was only five-two and couldn't weigh more than a hundred and ten pounds. Coop lifted her off the ground and hugged her. "Let's get outa here," he said.

He hailed a cab and told the driver to take them to a cheap restaurant—any cheap restaurant. He dropped them off in front of a Moroccan place named Couscous. It was a tiny establishment that in the U.S. would be categorized a notch or two above a dump. They had their choice of tables; none of the five was taken.

Zoe looked at the menu. "Any idea what's good here?"

Coop laughed. "One guess." He ordered two plates of couscous mixed with an assortment of grilled vegetables, then looked at Zoe. "Did you kill him?"

Zoe's eyes opened wide and her eyebrows lifted. "Me? I figured you did. Your picture is on every TV channel and the front page of every newspaper in Israel."

"Mizrahi was smoking a cigar and scarfing down the food you delivered when I left him in the prime minister's study."

"Well, if I didn't do it and you didn't do it..."

"Hold it, hold it. Let's back this up. What the hell are you doing here in the first place?"

"It's a long story."

"I've got the time."

The meals arrived but neither of them touched the food. "You remember the nine-million dollars I took with me when I left the Agency and ran off to Zurich?" Zoe said.

Coop rolled his eyes. "How could I forget?"

"You must have been disappointed with me."

"Not really. We had talked about you building a new life with Lara in Zurich."

"Still, we didn't talk about me taking the money to my new life."

"Look, only four people knew the money really existed: Randy, who is dead, McNamara who would take a lead bullet for you, and you and me. Hell, I figured you earned it."

"Well, I started feeling guilty. The money was sitting in an account earning five percent and I was getting rich just on the interest. I decided to give the money back to the Agency, but I couldn't figure out a way to do it without involving you in its disappearance. I was worried you would get hit with the blowback so..."

"So what?"

"So...I got in touch with an old contact in the Mossad and I asked if he'd help me get it back to the U.S."

"And why didn't he?"

"He did his best. A guy with credentials and documents who said he was Mizrahi's number one guy showed up at my door."

Coop took out a photo of Joseph Halevi that had appeared in the local newspaper. "This was Mizrahi's number one guy. Do you recognize him?"

"No, that wasn't the guy."

"You sure?"

"Coop, I worked for the Agency for twenty-three years. I think I know how to I.D. someone."

Coop stuffed the photo back in his pocket. "Yeah, sorry. So, what did this guy do for you?"

"He set up a meeting in Geneva."

"A meeting? With whom?"

"Mizrahi himself."

"Wow, talk about breaching protocol. Didn't that seem a little strange to you?"

"Yeah, it kinda did, but Mizrahi said he owed Director Dutton a favor and he'd get the money back to the Agency. He said he would personally make sure it got there without bringing up your name or mine."

"So you wired it to him?"

"Not directly. I routed it through a shell company in Cyprus. It was supposed to go directly from there to Mizrahi."

"Let me guess. The money got sent to Iran."

"Not only did it go there, but the next day I was on Mossad's Iranian operative hit list."

A waiter passed the table and Coop raised his finger. "Do you serve alcohol here?" he asked.

"Sir?"

"You know, alcohol...booze...spirits. Anything to calm the nerves." The waiter shook his head and scurried off toward the kitchen.

When he returned, he placed two glasses and a small carafe filled with an amber liquid on the table. "Arak, sir. Very strong." He filled the glasses.

Coop raised his glass. "Well, here's to getting outa this one alive."

They downed the liquor and Zoe made a face. "Tastes like licorice. I hate licorice."

Coop smiled and refilled their glasses. "So you went to Israel to confront Mizrahi?"

"Not just to confront him. If he stole the money, I was prepared to kill him. The only problem was when I made it into his inner sanctum, you were there."

The obvious crossed Coop's mind. "Are you sure you didn't go back later and do just what you threatened to do?"

"I went back, but he was already dead. His throat was cut from ear to ear."

Twelve

The news hit the Agency hotline early that morning and when Director Dutton checked in at seven a.m., there were already a dozen messages demanding return calls. The most urgent was from his boss, the director of national intelligence. He tapped his intercom. "Leslie, you're going to be getting a lot more calls this morning. Tell 'em I won't be in the office till noon...tell them I'll call 'em back."

"I understand, sir," she said.

Dutton looked through the Agency phone directory and dialed a number. The receptionist picked up on the first ring. "Deputy Cooper's office."

"This is Director Dutton. Is the deputy director available?"

"Oh, hello, sir. No, Deputy Cooper is on an assignment for a few days."

"Is that so. When will he be back?"

"Uh, I'm not really sure, sir."

"Okay, Miss...?

"It's Mrs., Mrs. Greene. You can call me Amy."

"Okay, Amy, if you want to be working there tomorrow, you better tell me when Cooper left and where he went."

Tears welled up in Amy's eyes. She knew she had made a promise she couldn't keep. "He...he left four days ago."

"And?"

"That's it. I don't know where he went."

"Are you sure?"

Amy broke into tears and had trouble catching her breath. "That's...that's...that's really all I know, Director Dutton. Pl.. please...believe me."

"Okay, I believe you. Who's in charge while Cooper's gone?"

"Agent McNamara, sir."

"Put him on."

Amy put Dutton on hold and scurried into McNamara's office. She startled him and he looked up from the document he was reading. His Irish complexion was ruddier than usual—closer to scarlet than red. "Amy, what is it?"

The receptionist was still crying and taking big breaths between words. "Coop is...Coop is..."

"Say it. Coop is what?"

"Coop is in trouble. Director Dutton's on the phone."

McNamara waved Amy out of his office and punched a flashing button on his phone console. "Director Dutton, this is Agent McNamara."

Dutton was not one to beat around the bush. "Why did Cooper go to Israel?"

"Your guess is as good as mine, sir."

"Goddammit, McNamara, since when does the deputy director just run off without telling anyone?"

"This is the first time, sir."

"Did you see that two-page communique from Mossad?"

"Yes sir, I was just reading it."

"Do you believe it?"

"That Coop killed Mizrahi?"

"Yeah, that."

"No, sir, I don't. Do you?"

"I don't know what to think. A week ago, we hear that someone with possible ties to a U.S. intelligence agency is being sought by Mossad for helping Iran and then Cooper sneaks off and is accused of killing their director. Something's not right here."

"Mr. Director, I know Coop and he's not an Iran sympathizer, let alone an assassin."

"Well, you get your ass over there and find him...and, goddammit, get him back here ASAP."

~ * ~

Coop was pretty sure his home phone would be tapped, so before leaving the restaurant, he talked to the owner for directions to the nearest internet café. They wandered around for a half hour and finally found it. It was packed. Tourists speaking a dozen different languages were waiting in line to get ten minutes on a computer with email capability. When they reached the front of the queue, Coop nudged Zoe forward and pointed to a vacant PC. "Go ahead. I'll wait."

Coop didn't ask, but he was positive Zoe was corresponding with Lara. She used the full ten minutes typing messages and reading responses and when she stepped away, her hand was trembling.

Coop took the empty seat and went straight to Google's mail page. He typed in Fran's address: **F, don't believe anything you see on the TV or in the newspapers. I got myself in the middle of a situation, but I'll work it out and be fine. Tell Josh I love him and still hope to be home for his first game. Love you too. C.** He waited for a reply, but there was none. Fran obviously wasn't at her computer and wouldn't see the email until later.

On the way to the light rail station, Coop jotted an address on a piece of paper and handed it to Zoe. "Here's where I'm staying.

There's an extra bunk in my room...you wanna be roommates again?"

"Do you still snore?"

"Fran says I do, but I don't believe her."

"Well, I'm going with Fran on this one, but I'll accept the offer if you promise it won't be for long."

"Let's hope it won't. Pick up your stuff and meet me there."

Thirteen

Zoe looked around the room and laughed. "What?" Coop said.

"It's been a long time since you and I shared bunk beds."

It was Coop's turn to laugh. "It's been a long time since we shared any bed."

"Romania?"

"No, Poland," he said.

"Oh, yeah, Poland, a lifetime ago."

"Actually, nineteen years ago."

Zoe shook her head. "Like I said, a lifetime ago."

Their reminiscing was interrupted by the squealing sound of a police siren. It got louder until it was right outside the building. Coop grabbed Zoe by the arm and led her to the men's communal bathroom. They both got into one stall. Coop sat on the throne and dropped his trousers so his shoes and pants could be seen from under the door and Zoe stood on the tank so she couldn't be seen at all. They waited for twenty minutes without hearing any activity on their floor. Coop pulled up his pants and Zoe jumped down. They exited the stall just as a young guy stepped into the room. He looked at them with disdain. "Hey, folks, you're too old for this. Get a room, for God's sake."

Coop gave the guy the finger and he and Zoe returned to their room. "So, who's the Mossad guy you reached out to when you decided to send the money back?" Coop asked.

"His name's David Blum. I worked with him on a case back in the nineties."

"Do you trust him?"

"Implicitly."

"Would you trust him with your life?"

"I did once and he came through."

"That's good enough for me. Do you have a contact number for him?"

Zoe tapped her temple with her index finger. "It's right here in my personal phonebook."

~ * ~

Mossad, the heart of the Israeli intelligence community, was located in Tel Aviv and that's where David Blum was stationed. Coop had just escaped that city and wasn't happy about going back, but he had no choice. He checked a local map and had Zoe set up a meeting for ten p.m. in Luna Park, an amusement area located in the Tel Aviv fairgrounds.

Zoe was certain Blum could be trusted, but Coop wasn't so generous. She arranged to meet Blum at the carousel ticket booth while Coop would loiter nearby next to an ice cream stand. If Coop was sure Blum didn't have any colleagues waiting in the wings, he would unwrap an ice cream bar and begin eating it. If something didn't look right, Coop would dump the ice cream into the trash.

It was Monday night, and by ten o'clock all the young kids were home in bed. Most of the carousel riders were around eighteen years old, who had just gotten the right to drink and had overdone the privilege.

Zoe looked at her phone. It was two minutes to ten. A guy with jet black hair and light blue eyes stepped into line behind her. "Ready to ride a wooden horse?" he said.

Zoe turned and smiled. "Don't you get any older? Where's the gray hair?"

"It's dyed. Hey, you look great. I always was a sucker for a blonde. Would it be appropriate to give you a kiss on the cheek?"

Zoe turned her head and David planted a juicy one on her. "I'll get us tickets."

She glanced over at the ice cream stand. Coop was taking a bite from a fudgsicle. "That'll be fine," she said.

A white stallion with a pink and blue saddle was poised and ready to go. Zoe climbed on just as the merry-go-round began to start moving. David remained standing and held onto a brass pole. "I guess we've opened a can of worms," he said.

"I'm in trouble, David, and so is my old partner."

"You don't have to tell me. Every Mossad agent is drooling at the mouth to get ahold of either one of you guys." He turned his head and scanned the surroundings. "I assume Cooper is nearby."

"He'll be here soon."

Almost on cue, Coop hopped onto the revolving platform and made his way to Zoe and Blum. He offered his hand. "Craig Cooper...call me Coop."

"Your mug shot doesn't do you justice, Coop. David Blum... nice to meet you."

Coop withdrew his hand and steadied himself against one of the stationary ponies. "So, David, let me draw this out for you. You have a man contact Zoe and he arranges a meeting with Mizrahi. After that meeting, Zoe wires Mizrahi nine million dollars, but it somehow ends up somewhere in Iran. Mizrahi thinks he was duped and he labels Zoe an Iranian sympathizer or worse yet, maybe a spy. Then, Mizrahi gets murdered and I get accused of being his assassin. Does anything in this picture look fishy to you?"

"I assume you didn't do it," David said.

"What would be my motive? And even if I had one, why would I do the dirty work? There's plenty of rent-a-killers around."

"Okay, I know Zoe and she's no Iranian spy, and I've heard enough about you to know you're no assassin. But, look, I just passed along Zoe's request for a meeting. What do you expect me to ...?" The carousel began to slow down and Blum's head instinctively turned. "Get out of here. Now," he said.

Coop didn't bother to look where David was staring. He lifted Zoe off the wooden horse and they both took off running.

Two guys, both carrying more fat than muscle, jumped from the platform in pursuit, but after a hundred yards they both pulled up and bent over with their hands on their hips. The big guy was sucking air like a man who had just been saved from drowning, and the shorter one looked like he was ready sink to the bottom for the last time. They trudged back to the carousel and the big man looked at Blum. "You...you let them get away?" he said.

Blum shook his head. "What the fuck do you think you were doing?"

"Our job...arresting spies and killers."

"I told you to keep your distance."

"Well, I made an executive decision. It was time to grab them."

Blum got into the guy's face. "I've got news for you. You're not an executive and you're not a decision maker." He put his finger into the guy's chest. "I make the decisions and you follow my orders."

The guy pushed Blum's hand away. "Yeah, well, you're going soft. Maybe it's time for you to retire."

Blum took a step back, cocked his fist and let the guy have it under the left side of his chin. The man fell to one knee. "Retire that, you prick," Blum said. "Now get the hell out of here before I think about telling Halevi what fuckups you are."

The big guy rubbed his chin. "But..."

"Now," David said.

The duo took off and Blum scanned the area, hoping he'd spot Coop and Zoe, but they were long gone.

Fourteen

McNamara checked the availability of the Agency jets. All the Gulfstreams were out of the U.S. except for one, which was reserved for domestic use only. Air France had a direct flight from D.C. to Jerusalem, but the Agency frowned on using foreign carriers, so he booked a first-class seat on a United flight that had a change of planes in New York City.

Mac's flight didn't leave for another three hours. He looked up Coop's home address and headed over to Arlington. It was dinnertime when he knocked on the Coopers' door. Josh opened it with a startled look on his face. "Mr. McNamara, is something wrong? Is my dad okay?"

McNamara put his hand on Josh's shoulder. "Everything's fine. Is your mom at home?"

Josh invited the agent into the living room and then went to find Fran, who was in the kitchen stirring a pot of spaghetti. "Mr. McNamara's here," Josh said.

Fran took off her apron and stepped into the living room. "Mac, is Coop all right?"

"As far as I know he is." McNamara patted the couch cushion. "Sit, we'll talk."

Fran sat next to McNamara with a feeling of trepidation. She knew what he was going to ask her, but she didn't know what her answer would be. If she told Mac the truth, he might get in Coop's way and make things worse. If she lied, he might be thrown off Coop's trail when maybe Coop needed some help.

"Fran, I want to help Coop. Where did he go?"

"Mac, I promised him..."

"I get that, but he's in big trouble. If Mossad gets to him before I do, he could go to prison for the rest of his life."

Fran rubbed her temples as if they needed a massage. "God, I don't know what to do."

"Trust me, please. I owe Coop my job. I want to help him."

Neither Fran nor McNamara was aware that Josh was standing in the hallway next to the living room until Josh stuck his head around the corner. "Tell him, Mom," he said.

Fran went to Josh and hugged him tight. "Honey, I don't know if—

"Just tell him. He wouldn't do anything to hurt Dad."

Fran returned to the couch. "Five days ago, Coop got a phone call from Zoe's partner. She said they were vacationing in Cyprus, when Zoe just disappeared. A few minutes earlier, Coop had read the memo about Israel cracking down on spies and he was sure the two events were somehow related. He took the Wainwright jet to Cyprus."

McNamara scratched his chin. "Any idea what he was doing in Jerusalem?"

"I don't know. Chasing Zoe, I guess."

"Has he contacted you?"

"He sent me an email. He told me not believe what's on TV or in the newspapers. He said he was working on straightening it out."

"And Zoe?"

"Didn't mention her."

McNamara stood to leave. "Look, Fran, I'm going over there to do what I can to help them. If Coop sends another email, see if you can find out where he is and tell him I'm on my way. I'll be in touch."

Fran saw McNamara out and turned toward Josh. "I think you were right."

Josh gave her a hug. "He won't be home for my game, will he?"

Fran showed a weak smile. "I don't know, honey. I wouldn't plan on it."

Fifteen

It was after midnight by the time Coop and Zoe got back to
the hostel they had checked into earlier in the day. It was cheaper
than the one in Jerusalem, but the sheets weren't very clean and
the water wasn't very hot. They flopped onto their bunks. "Do you
still trust Blum?" Coop asked.

"Well, yeah. If he was setting us up, he wouldn't have warned
us about those goons. I'm telling you, he's a good guy."

Coop tossed his burner phone to the top bunk. "Okay, call
him. Set up another meeting."

"For when?"

"Man, you've been out of the spy business too long. For
tonight."

Blum knew how good intelligence agents worked and wasn't
surprised when his phone rang at 12:30. He answered on the first
ring and gave Zoe directions to an all-night bar, Mondo 2000,
located in the artistic district. He said he could make it by 1:30.

It was a three-block walk from the hostel to a large boulevard
where they were able to hail down a taxi; from there to Mondo
2000 the ride took only about twenty minutes. Unfortunately,

Coop hadn't changed any of his dollars into shekels and the cab driver stuck it to him on the exchange rate. Coop retaliated and stiffed him on the tip.

Coop wasn't thrilled with the meeting site. Blum hadn't mentioned that Mondo 2000 was a rooftop bar. It provided great views of Tel Aviv, but not many exit routes for fugitives. He sent Zoe upstairs to scope it out while he remained on the street and waited for Blum to arrive. He didn't have long to wait; within a few minutes a taxi rolled up and Blum hopped out. He spotted Coop and gave him a subtle wave.

Coop peered up and down the street. It was crowded with young people who were either in pairs or looking to hook up. Other than him and Blum, no one appeared to be over twenty-five, so unless Mossad was hiring babies, he figured the coast was pretty clear. "Why here?" Coop asked. "It's a long jump off that roof."

"Look, Coop, either you trust me or you don't. I could be home with my wife right now, but I'm here instead. So, are we going upstairs or not? It's your call."

Coop made one last sweep of the street. "Lead the way."

The combination of soul and jazz the trio was playing sounded mellow on the street, but was several decibels louder when they stepped onto the rooftop. Zoe had chosen a table in the back where it was much quieter and much nearer to the rear stairway.

Zoe ordered a beer and Coop asked for the same. Blum opted for a plain Pellegrino. "Sorry about the fiasco on the carousel," he said.

"Who were those guys?" Zoe asked.

"They're Mossad, but they're legacies. If it weren't for their fathers, they'd be sweeping streets. Apparently one of them has a thing for roller coasters and they were playing hooky when they recognized you two."

Coop wasn't totally convinced, but let it go. "How far are you willing to stick your neck out?" Coop said.

"Try me."

"Okay, who did you send to talk to Zoe about transferring the cash?"

"I didn't send anyone. I contacted Mizrahi's deputy and he said he'd take care of it."

Coop took a pull off his beer. "And who was that?"

"Josef Halevi."

Coop cocked his head. "The guy who took over Mossad after Mizrahi was killed?"

"Right."

Coop turned to Zoe. "I showed you this guy's picture. Was he the one who came to your house?"

"Jeez, Coop, I told you already; it wasn't him."

"Any idea who put out the story that Zoe's an agent for Iran?" Coop asked.

"Well, it came directly from Mizrahi's office, so I'm guessing he did."

"And who put out the story that I killed Mizrahi?"

"That came directly from Halevi's office, so I'm guessing he did."

Coop drained the beer bottle. "Can you get me a passport? Say German or Dutch?"

Blum shook his head. "Look, Coop, I like you and I love Zoe, but my neck doesn't stretch that far."

Coop nodded. "I didn't think so, but it was worth the try."

Blum finished off his drink. "I have to get going. Is there anything else?"

Coop thought for a moment. "Do you know a Mossad guy named Lev Cohen?"

"Sure, I know him."

"Is he a straight shooter?"

"As far as I know, yeah."

Coop stood and shook Blum's hand. "Thanks, buddy. We appreciate your help."

It was almost three a.m. and the inventory of available cabs was dwindling. Blum yelled something in Hebrew to a driver who was getting ready to take off and the cabbie stopped. "You guys take this one. I'm within walking distance of my apartment," Blum said.

Zoe got in first and Coop followed, but before he closed the door he looked back at Blum. "Hey, David, I just thought of something else. Do you know an agent name Rachel? She works for Lev Cohen."

Blum laughed. "Her name is Rachel Kagan and she doesn't work for Lev. He works for her."

Sixteen

McNamara was bleary-eyed when he stepped off the plane in Jerusalem. Counting the layover in New York, he had been traveling for almost sixteen hours. He collected his luggage and hailed a cab to take him into the city.

The Agency people always stayed at the Jerusalem Hilton, but McNamara didn't want any of his colleagues to know he was there. The station chief was already seething that Coop had come to the city without notifying him and now that his deputy director was suspected of killing the chief of Mossad, he was infuriated that he had to give Coop cover with the press. Mac checked into the King David Hotel.

The long flight had given Mac plenty of time to ponder why Coop would have taken on this field operation without telling him or anyone else in the Agency. There was only one explanation: it was personal. He took it as a payback to Zoe for saving his life.

McNamara grabbed a power nap for forty-five minutes, showered and shaved, then searched through the contacts on his iPhone. He tapped in ten digits and hung up. Five minutes later his phone buzzed. "Is that you, C.T.?" Mac said.

"Yeah, who's this?"

"It's McNamara. Where are you?"

There was a long pause. "I'm in Cyprus."

"Is Coop with you?"

"No, why?"

"Why? Goddammit, C.T., you know why."

This was the moment C.T. had been dreading since reading the headline in yesterday's *Times*. "Listen, Mac, I don't know where he is."

"You flew him to Jerusalem. Right?"

"Yeah, I did."

"So, why didn't you fly him out?"

"The shit hit the fan over there and he told me to get the crew and the plane out as fast as possible."

"What else did he say?"

"He said, go back to Cyprus and wait for his call. If I didn't hear from him in a week, he said to head home."

"Okay, if he calls, you contact me. You have my number?"

"Yeah, it's here on my phone. I'll let you know."

McNamara was going to end the call, but on a hunch, he asked, "Did Coop have a contact in Jerusalem?"

"Yeah, a Mossad guy he buddied up to. A guy named Lev Cohen."

Mac was in a bind. He couldn't visit his station chief; it would tip him off that he was looking for Coop. He certainly couldn't contact Mossad; they would be in no mood to help him. So he called the U.S. embassy and requested a meeting with the ambassador. He checked the train schedule from Jerusalem to Tel Aviv—one every hour on the hour. If he could get to the station in ten minutes, he'd be in Tel Aviv in an hour and a half.

~ * ~

A Marine escorted McNamara from the embassy entrance to Billings' office and from there a secretary took him to a conference room where the ambassador was waiting. "Cup of tea?" Billings asked.

"Sure, what are you pouring?"

Billings beamed at the opportunity to show off his prowess of teas. "It's a Keemun from China—very rare." He poured a cup for each of them.

McNamara didn't know Keemun from Lipton, but said, "Wonderful. Let me cut to the chase here, Mr. Ambassador. Could you go through your channels to get me the contact information on a Mossad agent?"

Billings took a sip and dabbed his lips. "Absolutely, give me the name."

"Cohen. Lev Cohen."

The blood drained from Billings' cheeks. "This is about Cooper, isn't it?"

"Is that a problem?"

"If I get you what you want, you have to promise to keep me out of it."

"I don't get it. How could you be involved?"

Billings had the urge to add a little brandy to his Keemun from China, but he resisted. "I got Cooper and Lev visas into Lebanon. Do you think this Lev Cohen guy was Cooper's accomplice in the assassination?"

McNamara dropped his cup on the table without any finesse and stood to leave. "Just get me the contact info and don't be so quick to throw your own people under the bus."

~ * ~

Lev had been home recuperating since his return from the hospital three days earlier and only this morning was he able to dispense with the cane. This McNamara guy was right up front with him on the phone, by identifying himself as an Agency operative. Lev told him to drop by anytime. He showed up in less than an hour and Lev invited him into his living room overlooking the beach. "Nice place you've got here," McNamara said.

"Thanks. So, what can I do for you?" Lev asked.

"I'm looking for Deputy Director Cooper."

Lev smirked. "You and everyone else."

"I understand you spent some time with him."

"Yeah, I hitched a ride from Cyprus with him. He stayed here with me for a couple days."

"That so? What were you doing in Cyprus?"

"Same thing Coop was doing—looking for Zoe Fields."

"Really? Why were you looking for her?"

"Mizrahi sent me. He thought she was an Iranian sympathizer—maybe a spy."

"Did you find her?"

"No, neither did Coop. We thought she was in Beirut, so we flew there in Coop's plane, but we struck out. All that came from that trip was a bullet to my leg. Coop saved my ass. I couldn't believe he was just using me to get to Mizrahi and kill him."

"Don't you think you might be jumping to conclusions?"

"No. He was the last one to enter the study where Mizrahi was having dinner."

"Why would Coop want to kill him?"

"Beats me. Maybe to get him off Zoe's tail."

"So, where do you think he went after he killed Mizrahi?"

Lev smirked. "You're an Agency guy, if you don't know, nobody does."

McNamara thanked Lev and stood to leave. He handed Lev his card. "Here's my international phone number. Call me if you hear from Coop."

Lev hobbled to the door to see Mac out. As soon as he was gone, he keyed a number into his cell. "Rachel, a guy from the U.S. Agency just left. I think Cooper is still in Israel."

Seventeen

Mossad has been around since Ben Gurion established the intelligence agency in 1949, but Josef Halevi had only been the director for five days. He knew this was where he was destined to be. For years his inner feelings had been at war with each other, his pragmatic side telling him to wait his turn and his realistic side telling him to go out and make it happen.

He knew that early successes or failures could dictate his longevity with the 'institute' and he was determined to begin his era with a resounding success. Mossad would track down and arrest Zoe Fields, the ex-U.S. spy who had double-crossed Director Mizrahi by sending nine million dollars to Iran, and Craig Cooper, the rogue American intelligence operative, who assassinated Mizrahi.

The agents he chose to run point on the manhunt were Rachel Kagan and Lev Cohen. They were scheduled to meet with him in twenty minutes. When they arrived, Halevi greeted each of them with a handshake and a kiss on both cheeks. "Rachel, Lev, it is wonderful to see you. And Lev, how is the leg?"

Lev rapped his knuckles on his thigh like he was knocking on wood. "It's doing great, Mr. Director. Thank you."

"Please, please. In private we use first names, just as we have done for thirty years."

Lev smiled. "Thank you, Josef."

Halevi motioned toward a table and they took seats facing each other. He poured them each a cup of dark coffee and offered Rachel a piece of honey cake. "No thank you," she tapped her stomach. "Watching my weight."

"Are you sure? This is not from the bakery. My wife made it."

Rachel smiled. "Well, in that case, a small piece, maybe."

Halevi dipped his cake into his coffee and somehow managed to get it to his mouth before it fell apart. He turned toward Rachel. "Bring me up to speed on Fields and Cooper."

She politely pushed her plate aside. "Well, as you know, Fields was last seen in Cyprus, but Lev missed her by a day. Lev and Cooper went to Beirut looking for her, but she wasn't there either."

At the sound of Coop's name, Halevi shook his head. "We had no idea what Cooper was up to when he requested that meeting with Mizrahi?"

Lev joined the discussion. "We don't think he went there to kill him. We think he wanted Mizrahi to stop pursuing Fields and maybe when he wouldn't, things got messy."

"So, you have no idea where either of them is right now?"

Lev looked at Rachel and she gave him a nod to proceed. "We have a theory. We think Cooper found Zoe Fields and they're now travelling together."

"Travelling? Where?"

"Well, Cooper sent his plane out of Israel without him, so he must be travelling on his own passport. Which means he can't get out of Israel without being detained. We think they're moving around the country waiting for an opportunity."

"Do you think their ambassador might be the opportunity?"

"No, we're watching their embassy twenty-four-seven and yesterday an Agency guy named McNamara showed up in Israel looking for Cooper. If he finds him, he may find a way to get both him and Fields out of country."

"Do we have eyes on him?"

"Yes, but the Agency operatives are as clever as we are. He'll be hard to keep track of."

"You can have as many people as you want. Just don't lose him." Halevi stood and patted each of them on the shoulder. "I'm counting on you."

Eighteen

Most of the guests staying in the hostel were young people in their teens and twenties. Coop and Zoe stuck out like counselors at a kiddie camp. The sounds of flushing toilets and the odors from the communal bathroom woke them from restless sleeps. "We gotta get outa here," Zoe said.

Coop opened the window to let some fresh air in. "The hostel or the country?"

"Both," Zoe said, as she slipped out from under the faded sheets. She was only wearing a tee shirt and a butt cheek peeked out from underneath. Coop began to laugh. "What's so funny?" she asked.

"I was just thinking. Twenty years ago, that was sexy."

"And it's not now?"

"I still love you, Zoe, but it's different now. I'm married with a kid and you're in a long-term relationship."

"But those were great days, weren't they?" she said.

Coop cocked his head, trying to relive the times through his memory. "Yeah, they were great."

"Actually," Zoe said, "My long-term relation-ship may be getting shorter."

Coop nodded. "I sensed something wasn't right when Lara clammed up on me."

"What d'ya mean, clammed up?"

"She said you went to Cyprus to deal with a financial transaction, but she claimed she had no idea what it was. When I took issue with her answer, she got pissed and walked out on me."

Zoe closed her eyes and rubbed them with her fingertips. "I have to fill you in on a lot of details, but first I need a shower and breakfast." She picked up her bath towel and headed down the hall with the tee shirt still riding high on her backside.

Coop chose a coffee shop that served hot meals and he and Zoe took a booth in the back. Zoe looked through the menu and shrugged her shoulders. "Can you read Hebrew?"

"Let me see it."

She handed the menu to him and he skimmed the first page. "Try the shakshuka."

"You've had it?"

"Yup, cooked especially for me by a Mossad agent."

Zoe ordered the shakshuka and Coop opted for only a coffee and a blueberry muffin. "So, can you fill me in now or do I have to wait until you fill your stomach?"

"I think my stomach can wait." She took a sip of coffee. "When I decided to send the nine million to Mizrahi, Lara said it should go through an intermediary to cloud the paper trail. She told me how Swiss Commerce Bank uses a shell company in Cyprus and she offered to take care of it for me."

The waiter returned with the muffin and the shakshuka. "So, she not only knew about your financial business, she was involved in it?" Coop said.

Zoe took a bite. "Wow, this is delicious." She washed it down with a slug of coffee. "Oh, for sure. She was my agent."

"I don't get it. Why was she so secretive when I asked her about it?"

"Well, it's created a hole in our relationship. The money never got to Israel and instead it showed up in Iran. She thinks I blame her for the screw-up."

"And do you?"

Zoe thought for a long moment. "Yeah, I do, actually."

"You're not implying that Lara intentionally sent it there, are you?"

Zoe took another mouthful and stared off into space.

Nineteen

Six months earlier

Nikolas Georgiou's parents worked the land on their small potato farm sixty miles north of Larnaca. There was always plenty of food on the table, but there was never enough money left over for luxuries like new shoes or clothes. Nikolas wore the hand-me-downs from his older brother. He knew by the time he was sixteen that farm life was not for him.

Luckily the cost of higher education in Cyprus was supplemented by the government. Nikolas got a job ten hours a week as a bellman and was able to live in the big city and take a full load at Cyprus University. In June he earned a degree in finance.

The 2008 worldwide recession was in its second year by the time Nikolas interviewed for his first real job. The government wasn't hiring and all the banks were laying off, so he checked out opportunities in the private sector. There weren't many—two to be exact. The first was with a trucking firm that needed a bookkeeper and the second was with a company named Cyprus Exports that was looking for a junior controller. He took the position.

Nikolas never really understood Cyprus Exports' business plan. They had no warehouse, no trucks and only two employees. One was the controller, who stopped in every month to do a quick once-over of the books, and the other was Nikolas, the so-called junior controller.

His job consisted of sitting in front of a computer all day waiting for wire transfers to be reported. When one showed up, he was instructed to accept it and reroute it to a destination he had previously been given.

Nikolas was making a measly sixteen hundred Euros a month and was bored silly.

~ * ~

Kamran Rashidi hated his childhood. He was a product of the big city, where his father worked for the Tehran mayor as his number one gofer. He would be called out day and night, weekends and holidays. He always responded and strutted around town like he was a top dog.

His dad believed strongly in the patriarchal system; a social structure marked by the supremacy of the father in the family. It was demeaning to Kamran when his father would dress him down for a lack of ambition, and it was painful to watch his father berate his mother, but when his father informed Kamran's fourteen-year-old sister that she would marry a sixty-two-year-old widower, Kamran knew he could never survive in that family.

The mayor greased some palms on behalf of Kamran's father and got Kamran into Tehran University. He wasn't the best student, but he managed to struggle through in four years and to graduate in June. Two weeks later, his father told him he'd be working for the City of Tehran Office of Accounting as an entry level assistant to the treasurer. All day long he stared at a computer and kept track of the money that was wired from places around the world to Tehran.

Kamran hated his job and hated his father for putting him in it.

Twenty

The internet café wasn't as busy as the last time Coop and Zoe were there and the wait was less than five minutes. Coop held out his hand. "After you."

Zoe shook her head. "You go. I don't know if I really want to correspond with her right now."

Coop wasn't going to coax her. He took the empty seat in front of the computer. The last time he had emailed Fran, she wasn't at her computer so he didn't get a response. He was hoping his luck would be better this time. He typed in Fran's address: **Fran, are you there?** Their home computer chimed every time an email arrived and Coop hoped Fran would hear it. He gave it a few minutes and just when he was ready to give up the wait, an inbound email popped up: **I'm here. Are you safe?**

Coop typed quickly: **I'm fine. How are you and Josh?**

We're good. Did you find Zoe?

Yes, I found her.

Does that mean you're coming home soon?

Not quite. Zoe and I have to clear ourselves from these bogus charges.

I understand. Coop, you should know. McNamara is in Jerusalem. He wants to help.

That's good news. We'll try to meet up. Love to you and Josh.

Take care of yourself and come back to us as soon as you can.

Will do.

Coop stepped away from the computer and looked around the room for Zoe. She wasn't anywhere in sight, so he handed the computer off to a young woman carrying a backpack and a bedroll. He stepped outside and spotted Zoe at the corner. She was briskly walking away and he had to break into a jog to catch her. He yelled, "Zoe," but she kept right on going.

It took two blocks, but Coop finally caught up with her. "What's going on?" he said.

Zoe stopped and turned around. "Coop, I'm a lead weight around your neck. You have enough problems without trying to help me. I know how much you miss Fran and Josh. I can't …"

Coop took her shoulders in his hands and shook her. "Goddammit, Zoe, you're the reason I'm here. You think I could just save my own ass and hang yours out to dry?"

Zoe put her arms around Coop's waist and held him tight. "I love you, man."

"Yeah, I love you too."

They headed back to the hostel without saying a word. When they were back in their room, Zoe asked, "What's the plan?"

"We follow the money."

"It's gone. How do we follow it?"

"It made it to Cyprus. We start there." Coop looked at his phone. It was almost out of minutes. "Do you have any time left on your burner?"

Zoe clicked it on. "I've got about twenty minutes."

Coop held out his hand. "Let me borrow it." He tapped in ten numbers and hung up. Five minutes later it buzzed and he answered.

"Who is this?" a voice on the other end said.

"C.T., it's Coop."

"Oh, man, am I glad to hear your voice. Are you okay?"

"Yeah, I'm fine. Listen, did McNamara get in touch with you?"

"Yesterday."

"Where is he?"

"He's in Tel Aviv. He told me to get in touch with him if you called."

"That's great." Coop looked at his watch. It was almost noon. "Tell him to meet me at the Wishing Bridge at four o'clock."

"Will do. Should I still hang around here?"

"Yeah, I'm going to need your help soon."

"Gotcha. Watch your back."

Coop turned the phone off.

Twenty-one

Before McNamara left Jerusalem, he packed his carry-on and checked out of the King David. When he talked with Ambassador Billings in Tel Aviv, he was still lugging the leather case around with him. Billings suggested he stay at the Hilton, but McNamara didn't trust Billings and figured the ambassador probably wanted to keep an eye on him, so he headed directly to the Drisco—a hundred-and-fifty-year-old building that had been turned into a five-star hotel.

He was barely situated in his room when his phone vibrated. He looked at the I.D. and opened it. "C.T., what d'ya have for me?"

"Meet Coop at the Wishing Bridge at four."

"Anything else?"

"He told me to stand by and be ready to move."

"Okay. Thanks."

McNamara got a bite to eat in the hotel coffee shop and then stepped outside. It had begun to rain, and umbrellas were popping open on the street. He didn't have one, so he pulled his coat collar up behind his neck and did a three-sixty scan of his surroundings. He figured someone would be monitoring his comings and goings.

but nobody looked interested. Everyone was busy finding shelter from the rain.

A white Mercedes with a yellow cap on top pulled to the curb. The driver slid down the window and said something in Hebrew.

"Do you speak English?" Mac asked.

The driver nodded. "Yes, yes. Everyone speaks it here. You need a taxi, maybe?"

McNamara opened the back door and got in. "So, you get a lot of Americans over here?"

"Yes, yes, many Americans. Where to?"

"I kinda wanted to get a little sightseeing tour."

The driver looked annoyed. "There are many sightseeing buses in Tel Aviv."

Mac took out a one-hundred-dollar bill and handed it to the driver. "Just take me to a few spots until this runs out."

The cabbie shrugged, pocketed the hundred and pulled into traffic. He headed up Rothschild Boulevard and began pointing out famous buildings and museums. McNamara feigned interest for about fifteen minutes while he peeked out the rear window. He wasn't sure, but it looked like a silver Hyundai and a blue Volkswagen were switching positions behind the taxi every block or two.

The cab approached an intersection just as the light turned yellow; the cabbie drove through as it turned red. He looked in his rearview mirror and pulled to a stop near the curb.

"What's going on?" Mac asked.

"My engine light came on. It may be a problem."

McNamara looked out the rear window. The Hyundai hadn't made it through on the yellow and was waiting for the light to turn green.

The driver snuck a peek into his mirror and when the light turned, he said, "The engine looks fine, we go now." Mac looked back and the Hyundai was two cars behind.

Mac tapped the driver on the shoulder and pointed to a building in the middle of the block. "Pull up there," he said.

The cabbie looked confused. "That is just an office building. Not important."

"Pull over to the curb."

The driver did as he was told and McNamara watched the Hyundai speed by. He looked back. The Volkswagen was parked a half block behind. "You speak good English. Do you know what a prick is?" Mac said.

"Yes, yes. I know what that is."

"Okay, prick, give me my hundred back. I'm not paying Mossad for a tour of the city."

The driver handed the hundred back over his shoulder. "We're watching you, buddy, and we're going to find your friends before you do."

Mac snatched the bill and got out of the cab. Before slamming the door, he leaned in. "Yeah, we'll see about that. By the way, you guys are way overrated."

The rain began coming down heavier as McNamara weaved in and out of narrow side streets, looking back every minute or two, to make sure he didn't have a tail. By the time he was convinced the coast was clear, he was soaked to the bone. He looked at his watch; it was three forty-five. He made his way back to the boulevard, but all the taxis he waved at were occupied. By the time he got one to stop for him, it was after four o'clock.

The cabbie pushed down his meter flag and taking McNamara for an American, said in English, "Where to?"

"The Wishing Bridge. How far away is it?"

The driver pulled into traffic. "Fifteen, maybe twenty minutes." Unfortunately, traffic screeched to halt when a truck two car lengths ahead rear-ended a Metropoline bus.

~ * ~

Coop and Zoe split up. Coop sheltered under a tree ten yards from the bridge on the Kedumim Square side. Zoe loitered under an umbrella on the Peak Park side, five yards away from the wooden structure. They both had their phones ready to speed dial.

Because of the rain, only a couple people were on the bridge going through the 'make a wish' ritual. Zoe checked the time on her phone. It was after 4:45 and there was no sign of McNamara. The plan was to give him an hour leeway, and if he didn't show by five, they would assume something had gone wrong and they would scrub the rendezvous.

A couple minutes before five, Coop spotted a man in a pea coat with the collar up step onto the bridge and start across. Mac had red hair, but this guy's looked light brown. Coop wasn't sure. He hit send on his phone. "Zoe, check out the guy coming your way on the bridge."

Zoe pulled the umbrella over her head and took a few steps onto the bridge. The man was standing in the middle, but he didn't look like he was making any wishes. She kept the umbrella low and approached. The light was different from her side and his hair, although wet, was definitely red. She passed by and mumbled, "Irishmen are assholes."

The man didn't turn around. "Goddamn, I'd know that voice anywhere. How's it goin', Zoe?"

"It's goin' pretty rough. Follow me." She tapped her cell phone. "Coop, it's him. Make sure we're alone when we pass you."

Zoe walked by first and Mac was a few yards back. Coop went through his three-sixty scan and fell into step behind them. When they were two blocks away from the bridge, they stepped inside a coffee shop and the hugging began.

McNamara threw his arms around Zoe and gave her a bear hug that took her breath away. "God, I've missed you. It's been almost two years."

Zoe wiggled free and gave him a kiss on the cheek. "I've missed you too, Mac. I really have."

Coop, who was standing idle said, "Uh, hello."

McNamara laughed, turned toward Coop and gave him a man-to-man hug—a one armer. "Hey, boss. It's nice to see you too."

"You too, Mac."

They took a booth in the back. McNamara peeled off his wet coat and dried his hair with a napkin, while Coop ordered a round of coffees.

"Has the shit hit the fan back home?" Coop said.

"Let's say it hit, but it's not all over the walls yet."

"Is the director pissed?"

"Oh, yeah. He wants you home—pronto."

"Does he know Zoe's with me?"

"I doubt it. I wasn't sure myself until ten minutes ago."

The coffee arrived and everyone grabbed a cup to cradle in their frozen hands. McNamara took a big slug and let the hot liquid trickle down his throat. "Are you guys ready to go home?" he said.

Zoe shook her head. "I don't really know where home is right now."

Coop drained his cup. "Look, Mac, Israel thinks Zoe works for Iran and that I killed Mizrahi. We have to make things right over here before we can go back to the States. How long can you stall Dutton?"

"Geez, Coop. You know him, he'll be all over me in a week."

"Okay, we have a week then. Here's my plan."

Twenty-two

The flight time from Tel Aviv to Larnaca was an hour and five minutes. El Al Airlines had the most convenient flights, but McNamara wanted to stay as low key as possible. He chose a red-eye on the smaller Israeli airline, Arkia, and landed at 3:35 a.m.

When he stepped outside the airport the air temperature was pleasant, but the humidity made it feel like he had just jumped into a sauna. His light blue shirt instantly stuck to his back and dark sweat rings appeared in the armpits.

A lone taxi was parked next to the curb with the windows closed and the engine running. McNamara tapped on the window, but the driver was fast asleep with the A.C. vents pointed in his direction. Mac took off his shoe and banged on the window. "Hey, buddy, wake up."

The driver lifted his head and looked around like a bomb had just gone off. He spotted McNamara and jumped out of the cab. "So, sorry. So sorry, I took a cold pill. It put me to sleep. Luggage?"

McNamara threw his carry-on in the back and took a seat next to the driver. "You know where the Grecian Park Hotel is?"

"Yes. A very short ride. Sorry, I took cold pills, I..."

"Forget it. Take me to the hotel."

The ride took twenty minutes. Mac was sure the driver took the long way around, but the meter only read eight euros, so he gave him a ten and told him to keep the change.

He approached the front desk and asked the clerk to ring C.T.'s room. "Sir, it's four-thirty in the morning. Are you sure?"

"Just ring it."

C.T. was in the lobby within five minutes. "Mac. You didn't give me a heads up."

"Sorry, I was worried about the security on my phone. Where can we talk?"

There was an all-night coffee shop at the end of the lobby. C.T. tipped his head in its direction.

C.T. ordered an orange juice, but McNamara hadn't eaten since his meeting with Coop and Zoe. He ordered the American breakfast: eggs, bacon and fried potatoes. C.T. gave him a disapproving look. "My cholesterol's a little low. Trying to bring it up," Mac said.

"Well, that should do it."

The huge plate arrived and Mac dug in. With his mouth half full he said, "Coop needs his fake passports. They're on the plane... can you get them for me?"

"Sure, but where abouts on the plane?"

"He said the bottom drawer in the private bathroom."

"No problem. When do you need them?"

McNamara cranked out a quick timeline. It was almost five a.m. His return flight to Tel Aviv left at 6:40. "As soon as I get through with these eggs."

The cab ride to the airport took only ten minutes, validating Mac's opinion of his last driver. The Gulfstream was parked at the executive terminal, several hundred yards away from the commercial flights. C.T. showed his credentials and the two of them were waved through.

C.T. opened the Gulfstream's door and dropped the stairway. Boarding a plane with no power units operating is a strange experience—almost eerie. It was pitch black inside until C.T. hit a light switch that operated on battery power. He led the way down the seat aisle to the private bathroom Coop had used on the transatlantic flight. He opened the bottom drawer of the vanity, pulled out a pouch and handed it to McNamara.

Mac looked inside and approved of the contents. "Drop me off at the main terminal. I'm headed back to meet with Coop and Zoe. Coop wants you to fly to Amman and wait for us."

"Jordan? Why Jordan?"

"Since the events last week, a Wainwright Construction plane can't fly back into Israel, and after the fiasco in Beirut, it can't fly into Lebanon either, so the logical place is Jordan. We can get across that border by land without a lot of hassle."

"Gotcha."

Twenty-three

Zoe looked around the tiny hostel bedroom: a dresser, a bunk bed and one chair. The total square footage was less than two-hundred. "I thought we agreed to get out of this dump," she said.

Coop looked up from the list of notes he was making. "We will, but we can't right now.'

"Why?"

"Hotels require passports. Mine is on the hot list."

"We can use one of mine. I have four."

Coop hadn't told Zoe everything about the trip he and Lev had taken to Beirut, but now was the time to fess up. "When Lev and I were looking for you in Lebanon, I gave him a list of your phony passport names and their countries."

"So what? He couldn't have memorized them."

Coop didn't answer.

"You didn't," Zoe said.

Coop looked like the puppy who had just got caught peeing on the rug. "Yeah, I didn't ask for the list back."

"So he has my aliases."

"I'd say he does."

"Goddammit, Coop. That's not like you."

"Hey, I screwed up. I'll make it up to you." Coop's phone vibrated. He flipped it open. "Yeah?"

"It's Mac. I'm back. I have what you wanted."

Coop spelled out directions to the nearby coffee shop and warned him to make sure Mossad wasn't on his tail. He also told him to rent a car and pick up a road map to Jordan. He hung up and turned to Zoe. "Hey, get dressed, I'm taking you out for breakfast."

Coop and Zoe arrived first and were sipping coffee when a Mazda hatchback pulled up and parked next to a sidewalk that was marked by blue and white stripes. McNamara jumped out and locked the door. He spotted Coop and Zoe inside, waved and joined them at the table.

"How do you rate the preferred parking?" Zoe said.

"For a few extra shekels under the table, the guy sold me a sticker." Mac dropped the leather pouch on the table and picked up a menu. "What's good here?" he asked.

"Try the shakshuka," she said.

"Oh, yeah? You've had it?"

Zoe winked at Coop. "It's my favorite."

All three of them ordered Zoe's favorite. Coop turned the pouch upside down over the table and five passports dropped out: England, France, Germany, Canada and Gibraltar. He looked toward McNamara. "Did you bring the road map?"

"Oh, yeah. Almost forgot." Mac reached into his pocket and took out a thick wad of paper that had been folded over four times. He straightened it out and set it on the table.

"When will C.T. be in Amman?" Coop asked.

"He should be there by now, but are you sure you want to go all that way for a plane ride?"

"I'm afraid of Ben Gurion airport, Mossad will probably be crawling all over it." The meals had arrived and Coop was already into the egg portion. He used his fork as a pointer on the map. "Okay, here's Tel Aviv and here's Amman. It's about a three-hour trip, so if we leave in the next forty-five minutes, we'll be there by one. Another hour in the Gulfstream and we're in Cyprus before businesses close."

Zoe, who had been silent throughout most of the conversation said, "So I can't go with you."

"We can't risk your passport at the border, but if all goes well, we'll be back late tonight."

"And I have to hole up in that ten-dollar-a-day apartment?"

Coop squeezed Zoe's hand. "Fourteen hours, you've spent longer than that in a Polish prison cell."

Zoe pulled her hand away. "Yeah, yeah, don't remind me."

Coop thumbed through the passports and decided on Bernard Martin from Canada; he wouldn't have to affect an accent on his English. Inside of the passport was a driver's license with a Montreal address. Both the passport and the license had a picture of a young Craig Cooper smiling for the camera. He turned to McNamara. "Do you have a Canadian one?" Mac nodded.

He put the other passports back in the pouch and handed it to Zoe. "Take good care of these, will ya?"

"I used to be a spy, now I'm a clerk."

Coop frowned. "Hey, kiddo, are you really upset about this?"

Zoe smiled. "No, but I love giving you a hard time."

Coop paid the bill, gave Zoe a peck on the cheek and joined McNamara in the front seat of the Mazda. He took another look at the road map. "Okay, the shortest way is southwest past Jerusalem, but we can't take it."

McNamara started the car. "What? Why not?"

"We don't have visas to enter Jordan, so we have to go the northern route and use the Jordan River Crossing."

"I don't get it. What about the visas?"

"On that route, they let you buy them at the Sheikh Hussein Bridge before you enter the country."

"How much longer is the drive?"

"I'm not sure, but we have no choice."

McNamara shrugged, put the car in gear and headed for the Yitzhak Rabin Hwy, northeast bound. Once on the highway, McNamara kept the pedal to the metal while Coop kept his eyes peeled for any Israeli Highway patrol cars.

Coop checked the time; they had been driving almost two hours and signs were beginning to appear on the side of the highway. A road sign printed in Hebrew had the visual of a border crossing and 90 km printed underneath it. "We're getting close," Coop said.

Mac raised his sunglasses and rested them atop his head. "How long?"

Coop looked at the speedometer; McNamara was holding the Mazda steady at 130 kph.

He did a little quick math in his head. "We should be there in about forty minutes."

Thirty-five minutes later, traffic came to a halt and Mac fell into a queue behind a dozen cars inching toward the Sheikh Hussein Bridge and the Jordan River Border Crossing.

A huge parking lot came into view and a uniformed border agent directed them to a spot about twenty yards from a building where three white and blue flags were flying. Both men took one last look at their passports to make sure they had memorized who they were and where they were from.

"Are you ready?" Coop asked.

Mac slipped his passport into his pocket. "Yeah, I'm ready."

They stepped inside the building where people were queuing up in front of a half dozen booths manned by border agents. When they reached the front of the line, Coop went first. He handed his passport to the agent, who flipped through it and looked up at Coop to make sure he matched the photo. "What part of Canada?" he asked.

"Montreal."

"So, you're right on the ocean?"

Coop wanted to smile, but held it back. "No, sir. We're on the St. Lawrence River."

"Why are you going to Jordan?"

Coop pointed his thumb toward McNamara. "My buddy and I are tourists. We thought it would be a good day trip."

The agent leaned to the side for a look at McNamara. "Sir, could I see your passport?" Mac stepped forward and handed it over. "Are you also from Montreal?" the agent asked.

"No, Vancouver."

"So, you're right on the ocean?"

"Yes, sir. The Pacific."

The agent flipped through the pages of both passports. "Where are the stamps for your entry into Israel?"

Mac figured the answer was above his paygrade because he didn't have one. Coop took over. "We requested they not be stamped," Coop said. "We're going to the Arab countries after Israel."

"Can I see your entry visas then?"

Coop turned to Mac. "Did you bring the visas?"

Mac feigned surprise. "Me? I thought you did."

They began to argue until the agent interrupted. "Okay, okay, next time carry them with your passports. Are you driving a rental car?"

They answered in unison. "Yes, sir."

"The car has to stay in our lot, so you'll have to take one of the shuttles across the bridge." He stamped two cards, slipped them into the passports, handed them back and pointed behind him. "You can pay the fees and get your temporary visas into Jordan at that window. Next."

The shuttle dropped them off at the Jordanian border entrance, where they showed their visas and were waved through to a parking area. Several taxis were lined up and as soon as a driver spotted Coop and Mac, he pulled up next to them. "You would like a taxi? Yes?"

They jumped into the back seat. "How much to the Amman airport?" Coop asked

"Dinars or dollars?"

"Dollars."

The driver did some math on a piece of paper and held it up for Coop to see. "Seven, five." he said.

"Seventy-five?" Coop asked.

"Yes, yes, seventy-five."

Coop suspected it was a highball bargaining price, but they didn't have time to barter. He handed the driver a hundred-dollar bill. "Get us there in less than an hour and you can keep it all."

The driver made it in forty-five minutes and dropped them in front of a small private terminal located a block away from the commercial one. C.T. was waiting in front with a big smile on his face.

Twenty-four

Director Halevi was in a foul mood. It had been over a week since the former director had been assassinated and the suspects were still at large. He opened a pack of cigarettes. Most Israelis smoked American or English brands like Marlboro or Dunhill, but he preferred the Time brand, made right there in Israel. His intercom buzzed and he pushed the blinking red button on the console. "Yes?"

A voice came through the speaker. "Agent Blum is here, sir."

Halevi snuffed out his cigarette. "Send him in."

David Blum stepped into the office and approached Halevi's desk. "Nice to see you again, sir. Congratulations on your appointment."

Halevi waved off the compliment. "Please, David. I'm still Josef to you." He motioned to a chair facing him.

Blum took a seat. "Thank you, Josef."

The director shifted positions in his chair and looked noticeably uncomfortable. "David, I was given a troubling report involving you."

Blum didn't appear alarmed. "Really. What report was that?"

"Agents Klein and Feldman claim you had Cooper and Fields in your grasp and purposely let them get away."

"That's absurd. I told those pricks to stay in the background and instead they poked their noses in and spooked our suspects."

"I checked the old files. Years ago, you worked with Zoe Fields on a case."

"What are you implying? I've worked with dozens of foreign agents, that doesn't make me a traitor. You of all people should know that."

Halevi lit another cigarette. "So, you did meet with Cooper and Fields at the amusement park?"

"Yes, I did and those fucking idiots Klein and Feldman scared them off."

"Why would you meet with fugitives you know we are stalking?"

"Josef, it should be obvious. I want to know if there is a conspiracy here and, if so, how deep it may go."

"So if they contact you again, you will let me know?"

"Of course, if that is what you wish, but just arresting them right now will not bring resolution. We need the entire picture, not just a snapshot."

Halevi patted Blum on the back. "David, you're doing a fine job. I'm glad we had this talk. Give my regards to Maya. Tell her the four of us must get together soon."

Blum stood to leave. "I'll do that, Josef. Have a good day." He turned and walked out.

A side door to the office opened and Lev Cohen and Rachel Kagan stepped in. Halevi looked in their direction. "Did you hear all the conversation?"

"We did," Rachel said.

"Do you believe him?"

"He's hiding something," Lev said.

"Can we put a tail on him?" Halevi asked.

Lev laughed. "On Blum? He's a thirty-year man. He'd shake it in five minutes."

"What then do we do?"

Rebecca chimed in. "We concentrate on that U.S. agent, McNamara. He'll lead us to Cooper and Fields."

"Do you have him under surveillance?"

Lev raised his thumb. "Twenty-four seven."

Halevi ran his hand through his gray hair. "Very well. Keep me informed."

Twenty-five

A huge advantage of flying in a private aircraft versus a commercial one is the lack of border agents and customs inspectors one has to deal with. C.T. took care of everything. He collected the passports, knocked on the door of a small office and entered without waiting for permission.

Inside, the lone border agent was at his desk having lunch. C.T. handed him a bottle of twelve-year-old Macallan Sherry Oak Scotch, which he had taken from the Gulfstream's liquor cabinet. "Hey, Omar, a gift from my boss."

The Jordanian civil servant turned it over in his hands. "For me?"

"Yeah, he appreciates the good job you're doing here."

"Thank you, my friend. Thank you." He opened the bottom drawer of his desk and carefully set the bottle inside. "You are leaving?"

C.T. handed him the passports. "Yeah, these are the only passengers."

The agent gave them a cursory look and took out his stamp.

"Could you keep the stamps off?" C.T. asked. "These guys like to keep a low profile."

The agent handed back the passports. "No problem. You will return soon?"

"Probably tonight. Will you still be here?"

"That, maybe, will depend on how much Scotch you have in the airplane."

C.T. smiled. "We have plenty. See you later tonight."

Coop and McNamara were welcomed aboard by Josie, the flight attendant. "Good afternoon, gentlemen. It's nice to have passengers again."

"Hi, Josie. Getting bored, are you?" Coop said.

"I just like it when I know you're safe."

McNamara took a seat in the passenger compartment, while Coop went up front to the cockpit. The copilot was busy going through check lists while he waited for C.T. to board.

"How's the weather?" Coop asked.

The copilot handed Coop a computer-generated readout. "It looks like the isobars are converging quickly, which will probably set up a small hurricane in the Atlantic off the coast of Spain and Portugal. Then the counter-clockwise flow will work its way east over the Mediterranean."

Coop held up his hands. "So what does that mean in plain English?"

The copilot laughed. "I'd cinch up my belts real tight if I were you."

When C.T. had his flight plan filed and a departure slot secured, he boarded the airplane and saw Coop in the cockpit. "Hey, Coop, ready to go?"

"Yeah, sure. I hear there's some weather."

"There's a disturbance to the west, but Larnaca is only two hundred and sixty miles from here, so we'll only be in the air for about forty minutes. How bad can it be?"

Coop smirked. "I'll tell you in forty minutes."

The flight was smooth until they descended from thirty-one thousand feet through the clouds. Heavy rain pelted the aircraft and it was getting tossed around pretty fiercely by the wind. C.T. uncoupled the autopilot so he could hand fly the final approach and picked up the mic. "Hey, everyone back there. Tighten up and hold on."

Larnaca was using runway 04, which meant their heading would be to the north, but a westerly wind was blowing at twenty-two knots off their left side. C.T. turned the nose of the plane into the wind and approached the runway with his right wing aimed toward it. When they were a hundred feet off the ground, he kicked the right rudder, straightened the nose and set it on the runway with a thud.

C.T. picked up the mic. "Everyone okay back there?"

Coop looked over at a distressed McNamara. His complexion was a cross between gray and green and he was puking into a bag. "You all right?" Coop asked. Mac held up a thumb, but he wasn't very convincing.

Before they deplaned, Coop opened the gun safe and took out two Glock 23 pistols, each loaded with a thirteen-bullet magazine. He handed one to McNamara. "Will we need these?" Mac asked.

Coop slipped his pistol into a rear belt holster and pulled his shirt over it. "Maybe. Just follow my lead."

By the time they got into the back seat of the Mercedes, Mac was working on a sparkling water and was looking a couple shades better. Coop gave the driver an address. Fifteen minutes later, they were winding through a rundown section of the city. The cabbie pulled to the curb and pointed to a building. "This is it."

Coop and McNamara peered through the window. The building was unpainted concrete and two of its three doors were boarded up. The third had a sign on it: Cyprus Exports. In front of the door was parked a brand new shiny red Porsche 911.

They approached the building's door and turned the handle. It was locked. Coop made a fist and banged the side of his hand against it. No one opened the door. He banged it again with the same result. "Mac, rock that nine-eleven as hard as you can."

McNamara stepped on the bumper and began pumping it up and down. It only took two pumps before the Porsche's alarm began to blare. Coop took out his Glock. In less than thirty seconds, the Cyprus Exports' door flew open and a young guy in his twenties came rushing out.

He pointed at McNamara. "Hey, what are you do...?"

Coop shoved his pistol into the young guy's ribs. "Let's go inside," Coop said.

The three men went into the building. McNamara turned the dead bolt and took out his pistol. The young man was shaking uncontrollably. "What's your name?" Coop asked.

"N...Nikolas, Nikolas Georgiou."

"What are you doing here?"

"I...I work here."

Coop looked around the large room. Except for a desk, a chair, a file cabinet, a phone, and a computer, it was pretty bare. "Work? What kinda work?"

"Are you going to hurt me?"

Mac shoved his Glock into the guy's ribs. "Just answer the fuckin' question."

"I wait for wire transfers."

"Why?"

"They send me instructions...instructions to reroute the transfers."

"Who sends you instructions?"

"I don't know exactly. They come from the Swiss Commerce Bank in Zurich."

"Does the name Lara Graf sound familiar?"

Nikolas slumped into the chair. "I need...need water or something. I don't feel good." Coop looked at his eyes as they rolled up under his lids. He fell to the floor.

McNamara checked his pulse; it was racing. "There's water in the Mercedes. I'll get it," Mac said.

By the time he returned, Nikolas had his eyes open. Mac put the bottle to his lips and squeezed some water into his mouth. Nikolas began to cough and sat up. Mac handed him the bottle and he gulped down the rest of it. "Please, let me go home," he said.

Coop relieved him of the empty bottle. "How much do you make a month?" Coop asked.

"Uh, sixteen hundred...Euros."

"Is that your car out front?"

He winced. "Yes...sir."

"How much did it cost?"

The young man didn't answer. Coop pointed his pistol at him. "How much?"

"Seventy...seventy thousand."

"Euros?" Coop asked.

"No, dollars."

"Where did you get the money?"

Nikolas shook his head and wouldn't answer. Mac placed his weapon next to the guy's temple. "Where?" Mac said.

The young man began to sob and pointed to the front of the room. "A man came through that door. He handed me a briefcase and told me to look inside." He wiped his face with his sleeve.

"Did you?" Coop asked.

"Look inside?"

"Yeah, did you?"

"Yes. It was filled with cash—two-hundred and fifty thousand U.S. dollars. The man said it could be mine."

Coop took out the photo of Joseph Halevi that appeared in the paper when he was appointed Mossad director. He handed it to Nikolas. "Is this the guy with the briefcase?

Nikolas put on a pair of readers to get a better look at the photo. "No, I don't think so. I think the guy was younger."

"You sure? This isn't the clearest picture."

He scrutinized it again. "I'm sure. It wasn't him."

"Okay, what did you have to do to earn the money?"

"Was it yours? The money, was it yours? I'll give it back. I'll sell the car."

"What did you have to do?" Coop said again.

"Nine million dollars came in on a transfer from Swiss Commerce Bank. It was supposed to be routed to a man in Israel. I sent it to Tehran instead."

"I want the paperwork for that transaction."

"I...I can't."

"You can and you will," Coop said.

Nikolas wiped the sweat off his forehead, shuffled to the file cabinet and removed the upper drawer. He reached behind it and pulled out a manila folder that was attached to the back with duct tape. He handed it to Coop and Coop looked inside at the documents. "We're taking these. If anyone else comes looking for them, burn the whole file cabinet. You understand me?"

Nikolas's head moved up and down. "Does anyone else know about this?" Coop asked.

"No, no one."

"Do you have a roommate or a girlfriend you confide in?"

"No, I wish I did, but unfortunately I live alone."

"Okay, just keep your mouth shut and do what we told you to do."

Nikolas swallowed hard. "What about the money I took? Are you guys going to arrest me?"

Coop put away his pistol. "If you do as you're told, you can keep the money."

Twenty-six

C.T. landed the Gulfstream back in Amman a little after nine p.m. "How long can you keep the plane here?' Coop asked.

"As long as you want. The airport is getting six-hundred and forty dollars a day to park it. They'd love for us to stay a month or two."

"Let's hope it's only a week or so. Are you guys okay with your accommodations?"

"We're great...being treated like kings."

Coop handed C.T. the folder he had taken from Cyprus Exports. "Keep this in a secure place. I can't take it across the border, but I'll need it later."

C.T. hugged it to his breast. "Don't worry, I'll put it in the airplane safe."

Coop gave the crew accolades for the good job they were doing, while Mac rounded up a taxi to get them back to the border. It was waiting when they walked out of the terminal. The two men slipped into the back seat and the driver took off toward the Sheikh Hussein Bridge.

"I'm a better negotiator than you," McNamara said.

"Oh, yeah. How so?"

"I haggled the price. This cab ride is only costing us fifty bucks."

The Jordanian border agent looked at their passports. "You just arrived this morning and now you're going back to Israel? Why is that?"

Coop shrugged. "It was just a day trip. We did all the tourist stuff."

"So you were in Amman all day?"

"Yeah, all day," Coop said.

The agent stamped their passports and handed them back. "Good luck getting back into Israel."

Mac slipped the passport back in his pocket. "What d'ya mean good luck?"

"Just...good luck."

It was a short walk to the shuttle that would take them across the bridge to the Israel side. McNamara turned to Coop with a look of concern. "What did that guy mean by good luck?"

Coop shook his head. "Don't know, but it's my guess we're gonna find out."

It was getting late and there was only one Israeli border agent working. Unfortunately, it was the same one who had checked them out of the country earlier that morning. They handed him their passports and stood quietly while he examined them.

"Aren't you the guys who didn't have their visas with them this morning?"

Coop forced a laugh. "Yeah, that was us."

"That was a pretty short visit."

"Well, we just wanted to make it a day trip. You know, look around Amman, have a couple meals..."

"You spent the entire day in Amman, did you?"

"Yeah, checked out the mosques and the statues, mostly."

The agent tossed the passports on his desk and leaned back with his hands behind his head. "Which mosque was your favorite?"

"Uh...the big one, the big white one." Coop turned to Mac. "Do you remember the name of it?"

McNamara shook his head. "Not really. It had a bunch of Arabic letters printed across the front."

"Did you buy any souvenirs?" the agent asked.

"No, no souvenirs. It was only one day so..."

The agent pointed to a door behind him. "Step into that room, please."

Coop and McNamara started for the door, but the agent held up his palm and then pointed to Coop. "Just you."

Coop stepped into the adjacent room where a man looked up from his desk. He was huge, around six-foot-six and built like a tank. He removed a flashlight and a tongue depressor from a drawer and stepped in front of Coop. "Open your mouth," he said.

Coop opened wide and the guy shoved the wooden stick half way down Coop's throat while he directed the flashlight past Coop's tonsils. "Turn your head," the guy said. Coop did as he was told. The big man beamed the light into each of Coop's ears and jammed a Q-Tip inside. Then he stepped back. "Take off your clothes."

Coop's eyes opened wide. "Excuse me?"

The man pointed his finger at Coop. "You, you do not play games with me. You know what to do—strip."

Coop peeled off his clothes and stood at attention while the big guy examined every pocket, every seam and every button of his garments. "Hands on your ankles." he said.

Coop bent over and clutched his ankles while the man snapped on a rubber glove. The guy jammed his middle finger into Coop's anus and felt around for something—anything that didn't belong there. Coop winced, but kept his mouth shut. When the enforcer was satisfied, he withdrew his hand and threw the glove into the wastebasket. "Get dressed and send your buddy in here," he said.

Coop put on his clothes and left the room. McNamara raised is eyebrows. "It's your turn in the barrel," Coop said.

Neither man spoke until they reached their car in the parking lot. Coop put his hand on McNamara's shoulder. "Sorry..."

He waved Coop off. "Don't worry about it...comes with the job."

Mac didn't push the speed on the way back. So far, the trip had gone off with only one glitch and he didn't want to spoil it by being stopped by the highway patrol or local police. They pulled to the curb in front of the hostel just before one a.m.

Inside, two scruffy guys who looked like they were hippies left over from the sixties, were sprawled out on the stairs sharing a joint. "Hey, guys, mind if we get by?" Coop said.

Neither one even bothered to open their eyes. "Move," Coop said.

One of the guys sat up and looked at him. "Hey, Pops, did Big Mama let you out for the night?" Both guys laughed and they each took another hit off the reefer.

Coop gave McNamara a look that didn't need interpretation. Coop grabbed one guy by the collar and McNamara lifted the other by his hair. "On three," Coop said. "One, two, thr... The guys went tumbling down the stairs and Coop yelled back at them. "Tell your mamas they raised their sons to be assholes."

Several doors popped open to see what the commotion was all about. Zoe's was one of them. She shook her head. "You boys just can't stay out of trouble, can you?"

"Hey, Big Mama, did you miss us?" Coop said.

"Who are you calling Big Mama?"

Coop laughed. "Grab your jacket. Let's get a drink and talk."

The local bar was hopping. Coop ordered three beers and they took seats in a far corner. He wrote on the back of a napkin and put it in front of Zoe. "This is where your money went." *From Nikolas Georgiou, Cyprus Exports, to Karman Rashidi, City of Tehran Office of Accounting.*

Zoe took a pull from the bottle and looked at the napkin. "So, this Nikolas Georgiou guy sent it to Tehran instead of to Mizrahi. What did he get for his troubles?"

"Two hundred and fifty thousand."

"Who's this Kamran Rashidi that signed for it in Tehran?"

"We don't know yet, but my guess is he's also two hundred and fifty richer."

Zoe bit her lip. "How do we get to him? There's no way we can get into Iran."

"You still trust Blum?"

"Yeah, I do."

Coop raised his brows. "Okay, set up another meeting."

"You can't be serious. Now?"

"It's the best time. Nobody's watching."

~ * ~

Just like the first time they were there, Mondo 2000 was full of action: drinking, music and pickup lines. Blum was already seated at a table in the back when Zoe, Coop and McNamara walked in.

Blum gave a 'hi' sign to Coop and the three joined him at the table. "Who's the new guy?" Blum asked.

Mac offered his hand. "Name's McNamara. Call me Mac. I'm Coop's number one back in D.C."

"So you're sticking your neck out too?"

"Yeah, I am."

Coop passed the napkin to Blum. "Here's how the nine million dollars got to Iran. I have official documents locked in a safe that can prove it."

Blum looked at the handwritten napkin. "What's Cyprus Exports?"

"A shell company," Coop said.

"And who's this guy, Nikolas Georgiou?"

"He's just a puppet. Someone else pulled the strings."

"And you think Mizrahi's murder is connected to this money?"

"Think about it, David. That money was supposed to go to Mizrahi. It ends up in Iran and Mizrahi ends up dead. It's pretty obvious, isn't it?"

"Okay, let's say you're right. What do you want from me?"

Coop tapped the napkin. "This guy in Cyprus sent the money to Tehran and it was received by this man, Kamran Rashidi. The question is, where did it go from there."

"Maybe to the Iranian government."

"Maybe, maybe not. We have to find out where this Rashidi guy sent the money and to whom he sent it."

Blum shook his head. "I can't get you into Iran. You know that."

"Yeah, but I'll bet you know someone who can."

Twenty-seven

After returning from the meeting with Blum, and after McNamara left for his hotel, Zoe said to Coop, "This isn't going to work for me."

"What isn't?"

"You and Mac running around other countries trying to solve my problems. Look, you and I were partners in Iraq two years ago and together we busted our asses. We can do it again. I want to be part of the solution instead of just part of the problem."

"So, you want Mac out?"

"No, he's a great agent and loyal to both of us, but it's me I'm talking about here. I need to be on the front lines, not hiding out on the second floor of some rundown student hostel."

Coop knew Zoe well; she thrived on being in the heat of the battle. He smiled and gave her a high five. "Okay, partner, let's get this show on the road."

The address Blum had given Coop was in the south end of Tel Aviv, about a block away from the Central Bus Station. The neighborhood was the antithesis of the upscale areas that bordered the beaches, housed the hotels and featured the night spots. When

Coop and Zoe stepped out of the taxi, a young girl approached them and said something in Hebrew. Her outfit—short skirt, fishnet stockings and a sheer blouse—spoke a universal language.

Coop waved her off. "No, thanks."

"Come on, Mr. American, your wife can join in if she wants."

Coop gave the girl a closer look. She couldn't be older than sixteen. He took out two twenty-dollar bills and handed them to her. "We're not interested. Here, get yourself some breakfast."

It was close to four in the morning and all the businesses on the street had metal gates stretched across their entries. The address they were looking for matched a doorway to what looked like an American pawn shop. In front of the metal gate was a doorbell. Coop leaned on it, but no one answered.

Coop pushed the bell again and began rattling the gate. After ten minutes, a light turned on inside the shop, the door opened and a man stepped out and approached the gate. He was short—about five-foot five. He had long, blackish, gray hair and a distinctive Semitic nose with a mole next to his right nostril. His eyes sunk deep into their sockets and the left one was tearing. He yelled something in Hebrew that Coop was sure was an expletive.

"We're looking for Moses Rabinsky," Coop said.

"What do you want with him?"

"Blum sent us. David Blum."

"You work for the institute?"

"No, but we have money and we need Moses' help. Are you Moses?"

The man unlocked the gate and looked up and down the street. Except for the prostitute, it was empty. He motioned for them to come inside, then he locked the gate and closed the door. "My name is Moses, but in Yiddish I am called Moishe. It means delivered from the water."

"And were you?" Zoe asked.

"Was I what?"

"Delivered from the water."

"No, actually I was delivered from Chaim Sheba hospital. What do you want from me?"

"I want you to get me and my partner into Tehran," Coop said.

Moishe blinked and wiped the moisture from his drippy eye. "You are crazy, mister...?"

"Martin...Mr. Bernard Martin. Call me Bernie."

"Very well, Mr. Bernie. How much money do you have?"

"That depends. How much will it cost?

"Ten thousand dollars to me and twenty-five thousand to the man in Iraq who will get you across the border and into Tehran."

"How about getting us out?"

"Another twenty-five to him."

Coop knew he didn't have that much, but he wasn't going to blow the opportunity. "Okay, let me hear how you're going to do it."

"What kind of passports do you have?"

"We have them for several countries." Coop pointed to Zoe. "But hers may be compromised."

Moishe nodded. "I understand. I'll get her one to match yours. I assume you're not married, but we'll make it look as though you are. Can you get to Baghdad on your own?"

Coop ran a few scenarios through his head. "Maybe. I'll have to see."

"Very good. When you figure out how to get to Baghdad, I will get the passport for your Mrs. You pay me the ten thousand and I give you the cell number for the man who will get you from Baghdad to Tehran."

Moishe saw them out and locked the steel gate behind them. Coop looked around for a taxi, but at that hour in that sleazy part of town, none were to be had. They walked ten blocks north where they spotted a nightclub that was shutting down for the evening. Several people were lining up for cabs, so Coop and Zoe joined the queue.

On their way back to the hostel, Zoe confronted the elephant in the room, or as she thought, the elephant in the taxi. "Baghdad is six-hundred and fifty miles away; there's no commercial air service and private U.S. planes are banned. How are we going to get there?"

Coop had already given this question some thought. "I'm thinking maybe with the United Nations."

Zoe wrinkled her brow. "What? What are you talking about?"

"Ever hear of UNHAS?" Zoe shrugged her shoulders. "It's an acronym for 'United Nations Humanitarian Air Service.' It came across my desk about a month ago. The U. N. has begun flights from Amman to Baghdad exclusively for people working in the humanitarian fields."

"That doesn't exactly fit our M.O.," Zoe said.

"Well, maybe we can make it fit."

Twenty-eight

Coop threw his used-up burner phone into the Yarkon River and bought a new prepaid one with twelve hours of user time. His first call was to C.T. "Hey, Buddy, it's Coop."

"Hey, Coop, what's up?"

"Did you know Amman has a smaller airport than the one you're using?"

"Yeah, I think it's named Murka or Marka or something like that. A lot of the general aviation planes use it."

"It's Marka. Take a ride over there and see if any of the United Nations planes are parked there."

"Okay, then what?"

"Check out their logos. I want to cover up our Wainwright Aviation logo with one of theirs. How long would that take?"

"I don't know. If I hook up with the right guy and the right stuff, maybe twenty-four hours."

"Call me back at this number as soon as you check it out."

Coop knew it took money to chase money and he knew he needed more of it. He called Mac and told him to drop by the hostel for a brain-storming session.

Zoe was sitting around in a pair of short shorts and a tank top when McNamara walked in. He lifted his eyebrows. "Man, you look great, but aren't you dressing a little light? It's fifty-eight degrees outside."

Zoe rolled her eyes. "We don't have any control of the heat in this joint. It feels more like eighty-eight in here."

Coop looked up from a map of the Middle East he was studying. "Oh, hey, Mac. Can I get you something? Maybe a bottle of warm water or a hot beer?"

McNamara shook his head. "Sounds delicious, but no thanks. Why the meeting?"

"We're going to need a hundred thousand dollars to pull this thing off, but all I have left in my briefcase is six thousand. Can we finagle any money out of the Agency slush fund?"

"I don't think so."

"You sure?"

"Yeah, I'm sure. It would set off an alarm and Dutton would go nuts."

Zoe wiped her forehead with a towel for the tenth time. "How much did you say you need?"

"A hundred thousand," Coop said.

"I can get it."

"Where?"

"I told you the nine million has been making five-and-a-half percent for the last two years. Do the math."

Coop didn't trust his brain so he scribbled a few numbers on a pad. "Hey, that's about a million dollars. Are you sure you want to tap it?"

"Look, I got us into this mess, the least I can do is chip in a few bucks to get us out of it."

"How are you going to get ahold of it?" Mac asked. "You can't just have it wired to Zoe Fields, care of a local bank. Mossad would be there when you pick it up."

The three of them sat silent while their brain gears meshed. "What about Lara's shell company in Cyprus?" Coop said.

"What about it?" Zoe asked.

"What if Lara wires the money to that Nikolas guy and he wires it to my Canadian alias at an Israeli bank?"

Zoe thought about it. "Lara's not a co-signer on my account. She can't get to my money even though it's in her bank."

"She's a vice-president. Trust me, she can make it happen," Coop said. Zoe didn't respond. "Zoe, what is it?" he asked

Zoe stared off into the distance. "I'm not sure she'll go out on that limb for me." Nobody asked why. "The last time we communicated, I all but accused her of purposely sending that money to Tehran."

"Did she?" Mac asked.

"I don't really know."

"Then, this will be a good test. If she hung you out to dry before, she won't come through for you now. But if she does, you might want to cut her some slack."

~ * ~

The internet café was empty; Zoe settled in behind a PC while Coop looked over her shoulder. She typed in Lara's personal email address and then the message: **Are you there?** They both stared at the screen, but no response appeared. **Lara, are you there? It's important**, Zoe typed. They waited five more minutes before Zoe turned off the computer.

"Let's get a coffee and check again in a half hour," Coop said.

They sat at a small table and nursed a couple cappuccinos. Zoe didn't initiate any conversation, so Coop figured he'd open one. "You're worried she's stonewalling you, aren't ya?"

"Yeah, I am."

"Look, she's a busy woman. She doesn't sit at her computer all day just waiting for emails."

"I was hoping she'd be waiting for one from me."

"Finish that coffee and check your inbox."

Zoe pushed the coffee aside and went back to the computer She typed in her email address and waited. The page lit up with the message: **INBOX - 1 message**. She clicked on the message: **Are you all right?**

Zoe typed: **I'm fine.** Lara came back**: I'm sorry my Cyprus company got you in trouble.** Zoe typed: **That's in the past. need your help now.** The response came back: **Whatever you need.**

"Okay," Coop said. "Ask her to tap your account for a hundred thousand."

Zoe typed: **Take $100,000 out of my personal account and wire it to Cyprus Exports.** Lara responded: **Then what?**

Coop handed Zoe his Canadian passport. "Have Cyprus route it to the AIBC Bank branch on Rothschild Boulevard with this name as the recipient." She typed in the information and Lara responded: **It will be there this afternoon. Will you come back to me when this mess is over?** Zoe didn't respond and closed the computer.

Twenty-nine

Coop went back to the hostel to freshen up. He looked in the mirror; his facial hair hadn't been trimmed since his last shave on the Gulfstream ten days ago. He didn't dare cut it off for fear of being recognized, so he used a manicure scissors and evened it out. The best-looking pants he could dig up were a semi-wrinkled pair of wash and wear khakis. He put them on with a clean polo shirt that was pressed against the bottom of his duffel.

Coop knew the Anglo Israeli Banking Corporation is one of the largest banks in the world and that it specialized in international monetary transactions. If any bank could move money through in one day, they certainly would be the one to do it.

The AIBC branch on Rothschild Boulevard exuded wealth and old money. He glanced around the room. It was in the shape of a rotunda, and a glass dome allowed natural light to stream through. There were twelve desks for the executives, who ranged in age from their late thirties to their middle sixties; they were all wearing three-piece piece suits that resembled ones Coop had seen a few years back on Oxford Street in London. Coop decided to go for a rookie and picked out the youngest guy in the room. The exec greeted him in Hebrew.

"English?" Coop said.

"Yes, of course." He thrust out his hand. "Aaron Glaser, what may I do for you, sir?"

"I'm expecting a wire transfer today and I'd like to set up an account to receive it."

The young exec was ecstatic. His bonus was based on how many new accounts he brought in. He offered Coop a seat and asked for his ID. Coop handed him his Canadian passport and the Montreal driver's license. Glaser jotted down the numbers and gave Coop a form to fill out.

"If I may ask, what business are you in, Mr. Martin?"

"Import, export," Coop said.

"Ah, very nice. So this wire transfer will be coming from where?"

"Cyprus. A company named Cyprus Exports."

Aaron wanted to continue small talk, but was careful not to pry into his new client's personal business. "I wasn't aware Cyprus exported many goods."

Coop looked up from the documents he was filling out. "Oh, yes, figs. Cyprus dried figs are quite a delicacy on the island."

The young man lifted his eyebrows and shook his head. "Good to know. What denomination do you wish to open the account with?"

Coop had anticipated this question; he brought five of his six thousand remaining dollars with him. He set a stack of fifty, one-hundred-dollar bills on the desk. "I hope you don't mind, my business deals in cash."

Aaron began counting the bills. "No problem. Cash is king, as they say."

Coop handed back the completed papers, all of which contained fictitious names and addresses. "What time do you close?" he asked.

"Six-thirty."

~ * ~

Lev threw the gum wrappers and coins on the closet floor as he rummaged through the pockets of his dirty clothes. He knew it had to be there somewhere. He was about ready to give up when he spotted his torn, blood-stained khakis in the corner. He reached into the front pocket and pulled out a crumpled piece of paper. He flattened it out on the floor and read Coop's handwritten words: Zoe Fields, USA, Frieda Warner, Germany, Anna Tavros, Cyprus, Olivia Lee, Singapore.

He ran the names through Passport Control and got a hit. Anna Tavros from Cyprus entered Israel ten days ago, but never left the country. Lev was pretty sure Coop didn't have access to any of his false passports, other than the Arthur Wainwright one he had showed to Lev on their trip to Beirut. Passport Control hadn't recorded an exit for either Craig Cooper or Arthur Wainwright, so he assumed Coop was also still in the country.

Lev was certain McNamara had made contact with Coop and Zoe, but his Mossad agents were never able to keep track of him. McNamara knew he was being followed and always took the measures needed to shake them off his tail. Lev felt it was worth at least one more try.

~ * ~

Cooped checked his watch; it was ten minutes after six. He stepped into the bank and went straight to Aaron Glaser's desk. The young man saw him approaching and stood to greet him. "Mr. Martin, what can I do for you?"

"Did my wire transfer arrive?"

Aaron provided a wide smile. "Yes, yes it did and it's safely in your account."

Coop placed his briefcase on the desk. "Wonderful," he said. "I'd like to withdraw it. In cash, please."

Aaron's eyes looked like they might pop from their sockets. "Cash? Now?"

Coop opened the lid of his case. "Yes, please. Just place it in here."

"But, but Mr. Martin, the bank closes in fifteen minutes."

"I understand, but it's open now, so if you don't mind, I'd like my withdrawal."

Aaron placed a finger in the air. "One moment," he scurried off to talk to one of the older executives. A gray-haired man in an Oxford Street suit accompanied Aaron back to his desk. "Good evening, Mr. Martin. Mr. Glaser has relayed your request to me."

"Is there a problem?" Coop said.

"Actually, there is. We would have to open the vault to get that much cash. Perhaps tomorrow morn..."

Coop interrupted. "This is the Anglo Israeli Banking Corporation, is it not?"

"Yes, of course..."

"Certainly, you've handled much larger and more complicated transactions than this one." Coop's eyes narrowed and he stepped closer to purposely invade the man's comfort zone. "I want my money now. I can wait."

Beads of perspiration dotted the older man's forehead. He looked around the room for help, but all of the other executives had locked their desks and headed out the door. "Very well," he said. "I'll have the money brought up."

Coop stepped back. "And I want my initial deposit also. I'm taking my business elsewhere."

Thirty

C.T. had the Gulfstream parked about twenty miles south of the city at Amman's big airport, Queen Alia International. Marka airport, the smaller one where the U.N. planes were based, was only three miles from the city center. C.T. took a taxi.

He showed his pilot credentials to the guard and walked out onto the tarmac. A couple dozen small single and twin-engine planes were tied down to the blacktop, and five private jets, similar to the one he was flying, were parked near the terminal.

Fifty yards to the north were three large hangars. He took a stroll toward them. Two hangars had their doors open and he could see inside where maintenance crews were busily working on aircraft. The third hangar had its large sliding doors closed and locked. C.T. walked to the rear of the building. As he suspected, there was a small door with a window. He rubbed the dust off the glass with his shirt sleeve and cupped his hands near his temples to get a look inside.

Two jets he easily recognized as Brazilian-made Embraer 135s were parked side by side. They both were painted solid white,

just like his Gulfstream, and both had a simple logo that read: **UN**
He punched in Coop's burner cell number.

"What did you come up with?" Coop asked.

"I'm staring at two of their planes and they have really simple logos—just the initials U and N."

"Can you have some made?"

"I can buy them off the shelf."

"Yeah, but how will you attach them?"

"Ever hear of speed tape?"

"What kinda tape?"

"Speed. It's aluminum tape that's used for minor repairs to the skin of airplanes and race cars."

"Can you get some?"

"I'm sure I can buy a roll right here from the maintenance people, but if I remember right, it costs about seven-hundred dollars a roll."

Coop thought about it. The money from Zoe's account would easily cover it. "Will one roll do it?"

"I think it will."

"Okay, get the numbers and the tape and move the Gulfstream over to Marka airport."

~ * ~

Coop and Zoe took a cab back to the south end of Tel Aviv. The neighborhood didn't look any better in the daylight; it still had the seedy look of a red-light district.

The metal gate in front of Moses Rabinsky's office was locked. Coop rang the bell three times before the door opened and Moishe peeked out. "Is that my Canadian friend and his wife?" he asked.

"Soon to be wife," Coop said.

Moishe unlocked the gate. "You have the money?" Coop held up a paper bag. "Please, come in," Moses said.

Zoe wrinkled her nose. The office smelled like old socks. "What are you cooking?" she asked.

Moishe smiled wide. His teeth were stained from nicotine. "My wife...she's making gefilte fish. Would you like a little taste?"

"No, we just ate," Zoe said. "But it smells delicious."

"So, may I see the money?" Moishe said.

Coop handed the paper bag to Moishe, who emptied it on a table and counted out a hundred one-hundred-dollar bills. He turned to Zoe. "Do you have one of your old passports?"

She handed over all four of them and he examined each with a magnifying glass. "I will use this old photo from the Singapore passport. It will transfer easily to a new one."

Moishe turned to Coop. "And your Canadian passport, please." Coop handed it to him. "Come back in one hour," Moshe said.

A four-block walk got them out of the sleazy area where they found a street vendor selling food. They picked up a couple pitas stuffed with falafels and veggies and sat on a nearby bench to eat them.

"Zoe took a big bite and washed it down with a gulp of water from a bottle they were sharing. "Coop, is this going to work?"

"Is what going to work?'

"Following the money. Risking our lives in Iran."

"We have no choice. This whole mess is about the money. We have to find out where it ended up and who has it."

They finished off the food and headed back to Moishe's place. He was beaming and his bad eye had stopped tearing. "Some of my best work," he said. Zoe smelled fish on his breath.

They looked at Zoe's new passport. She was now Leslie Martin, Canadian citizen and wife of Bernard Martin. "Looks great," Coop said. "So how do we meet our contact in Baghdad?"

Moishe handed him a piece of paper. "This is his cell number. He will take over from there."

They walked back toward the food vendor and hailed a cab. Coop called C.T. but reached his pager. He tapped in his number and a few minutes later his phone buzzed.

"Sorry, I was picking up the stuff," C.T. said.

"No problem," Coop said. "Did you get everything?"

"Yeah, and only had to pay five hundred for the tape."

"Great, can you make the logo switch?"

"Piece of cake."

"Okay, tomorrow the border between Israel and Jordan opens at five a.m. We should be at Marka airport within an hour, so be ready to take off at six."

Thirty-one

It was after midnight by the time Coop and Zoe stuffed their belongings into their duffels and checked carefully for anything they may had left behind. They wouldn't be returning to the hostel.

They stepped outside to wait. It was a cool night, even for December; every time they exhaled, their breath formed little puffs of fog. Zoe rubbed her hands together trying to keep them warm. "What time did Mac say he'd be here?" she said.

"Eleven-thirty. He's late."

By twelve-thirty Coop was sure that something had gone wrong.

~ * ~

McNamara knew he was being followed. There were no cars in his rear-view mirror, but every few blocks he noticed a green Toyota and a white Honda alternated stop sign positions as he passed through the intersections. He made several turns, right at one intersection, left at the next, but those same two cars kept appearing. He tapped Coop's burner number into his phone.

Coop picked up as soon as it vibrated. "Mac, what's wrong?"

"I've got a tail on my ass that I can't shake."

"Where are you now?"

Mac looked at the street sign. "I'm on the west side of Nordau Boulevard near the kiosk."

Coop thought for a moment. "Okay, do you remember what we did in Brazil when we had this same problem?"

Mac chuckled. "Oh, you mean the São Paulo shuffle?"

"That's it."

Mac spotted a parking spot. "I'm parking the car right now. It's the same Mazda we took to Jordan." He slipped the keys under the floor mat and stepped out of the car. He looked behind him. Neither the Toyota nor the Honda was in sight, but he knew they were watching.

~ * ~

Coop motioned to Zoe. "Grab your duffel, we have to find a taxi."

They made their way to the main drag where the night life was beginning to light up. Zoe waved at a cab, but it looked like the driver had no intention of stopping for them. She stepped into the street and held up her hand like a traffic cop. The taxi screeched to a halt. The driver jumped out and began cursing in Hebrew. Coop dangled a hundred-dollar bill in his line of sight. He immediately calmed down and opened the back door for Zoe to get in.

Coop tossed the two duffels into the back seat next to Zoe and he took the passenger seat up front. "You know where the kiosk on Nordau Boulevard is?" he asked.

The driver gave him a disgusted look. "I am a cab driver in Tel Aviv. What do you think?"

"Sorry, of course you do. Drop us there."

~ * ~

McNamara took off on foot. Up ahead, a group of people, mostly in their early twenties, were mingling outside a bar where speakers were blaring out a Bruno Mars ballad. He stepped inside and ordered a beer.

He nursed his drink for ten minutes as he kept an eye on the street. It was hard to get an unobstructed view with all the people socializing outside, but he thought he spotted a green Toyota passing slowly in front of the bar. He left a ten for the bartender, stepped outside and weaved his way through the crowd; then continued on down the street.

Mac glanced behind him. It looked like a young man and young woman had left the bar scene and were walking arm in arm; every few steps they'd stop and kiss. He took a right at the corner and broke into a jog. When he looked back again, the lovers were walking faster and kissing less. He smiled and slowed his pace to a leisurely stroll.

~ * ~

The cabbie pulled to a stop next to the kiosk and flipped a switch to freeze the meter. It read thirty-five shekels, which Coop figured was close to ten U.S. dollars. He handed the driver a twenty and told him to keep the change. The man examined the bill as if it were counterfeit.

"Is there a problem?" Coop asked.

"The bill you held up on the street was a hundred."

"Yeah, that one was to get your attention. This one is for the ride."

Zoe pointed down the street. "There's the Mazda."

Coop grabbed the duffels from the back seat at the same time as the driver sped off. "Guess he's pissed," Coop said.

Zoe laughed. "Screw 'im."

The keys were under the mat, just as Mac said they would be. He also left a road map on the passenger seat. Coop threw the bags in the hatchback and slipped into the driver's spot. Zoe rode shotgun.

~ * ~

McNamara spotted a bench up ahead and took a seat. The young lovers approached going through the same kissy-face antics they had gone through for the last few blocks. When they reached

Mac, he realized they weren't that young; both looked to be in their middle forties. "Can you give me a ride back to my hotel?" Mac asked.

"Excuse me?" the guy said.

"In the Toyota. The one that's following us."

The young woman dispensed with the charade. "I suggest you tell Cooper and Fields to come into our office. We want to hear their side of the story."

McNamara smirked. "Oh, you'll hear it all right, but not until they want you to. So, do I get that ride or not?"

The woman looked at her partner and he jerked his head toward the street. "Sure, follow us," he said.

Thirty-two

Just as he and McNamara had done a few days earlier, Coop headed northeast on the Yitzhak Rabin Hwy. He looked at the time; it was close to two-thirty. If all went well, they would be at the Jordan River Border Crossing when it opened at five.

"So, do you think you'll go back to Zurich when this mess is over?" Coop said.

"Will it ever be over?"

"Of course it will."

"Well, if it doesn't end with a bullet in the back, I'll think about it."

Coop was quiet for a few minutes, then said, "I'm still not sure what role Lara played in this whole thing and why she called me if she already knew where you had disappeared to."

"Her shell company screwed up the money transfer and she felt responsible. She begged me not to go to Israel for fear I'd be killed, but I needed to know where that money was. I think she was scared. She must have felt you were the only one that could save me from a disaster."

"So why did she lie to me?"

Zoe shook her head. "Pride, I guess. Nobody wants to look like a fool."

"Yeah, I guess."

There was no conversation for the next twenty miles until Zoe said, "How's Fran and Josh?" Coop bit his lip and didn't answer. "Did I strike a nerve?" Zoe asked.

"Kinda. They're both okay, but I'm a shitty father."

"Why do you say that?"

"I just keep making promises I can't keep. A couple of weeks ago, I promised Josh I'd be back for his first basketball game. The game is in two days."

"Is Fran mad?"

"No, she understands, but Josh is only thirteen. I'm not sure he does."

"Give him a little more credit. He's a smart kid, he'll understand."

Coop sighed. "I hope."

Other than a few semis headed east, the traffic was sparse. In a little over two hours the border crossing signs began to appear. When they reached the parking lot at the Sheikh Hussein Bridge, Coop pulled in fifty yards away from the border agent building and checked the time; it was five minutes to five. He handed Zoe her passport. "Make sure you have it memorized. Do you remember our spiel?" Zoe lifted her thumb.

A uniformed guard opened the doors at exactly five, but Coop and Zoe didn't want to be the first inside. They waited for a dozen people to go ahead before they stepped in and joined the back of the line.

When it was their turn to approach a window, Coop spotted the same agent he and Mac had a few days earlier. He nudged Zoe in the direction of another window.

This agent took their passports and checked their faces against their photos. He looked at Coop and squinted. "Where were you born, Mr. Martin?"

"Montreal."

He looked at Zoe. "Were you born in Montreal also, Mrs. Martin?"

"No, Quebec City, sir."

"That's on the ocean, isn't it?"

Coop had prepped her for this one. "No, sir, it's on the St. Lawrence River."

He looked back at Coop. "Did you bring your Israel entry visas with you?"

Coop hung his head. "No, I forgot them."

"I can't let you through, you know that?"

"Yeah, I'm sorry. I realized I'd forgotten them, but we were two hours away from our hotel in Tel Aviv, so…"

"Well, I am sorry too, but you will have to go back for them."

Zoe broke into tears. "Sir, p…please. We leave for Canada in two days. If we have to drive back to Tel Aviv now…" she blew her nose on a tissue. "…we'll never make it back here. Please…"

The agent tossed the passports back to Coop. "You're lucky you're not Americans or I wouldn't have done this. Head to the shuttle and have a nice time in Jordan."

They bought their visas for Jordan at the next window and boarded the shuttle to take them across the bridge. "What d'ya think his beef is with America?" Zoe said.

"Who knows. The U.S.-Israeli marriage has always been a rocky one. Maybe he wants a divorce."

On the other side of the bridge, the Jordan agents waved them through to the parking lot. A taxi was on them immediately; they got in the back seat. "Marka airport," Coop said.

C.T. greeted them when they stepped from the cab. "We're ready to go," he said. "I have the crew with me, but I didn't know if you'd want Josie to pick up any food."

"No, we won't need any cabin service on this one. She can just come along for the ride." Coop looked at the logo as he boarded. "Looks great," he said.

The pilot grinned. "My mom wanted me to be a graphic artist."

C.T. joined the copilot in the cockpit and they went through the final checklists before starting the engines. When all the gauges were in the green, he keyed his mic. "Marka ground, Gulfstream Six Eight Seven Charlie Alpha ready to taxi...and ready to copy clearance to Baghdad International."

The copilot copied the instructions as C.T. taxied and joined the takeoff lineup. Ten minutes later the tower radioed, "Seven Charlie Alpha cleared for takeoff. Have a good flight."

In less than an hour and twenty minutes, C.T. began a descent and radioed the tower. "Baghdad tower, good morning. United Nations Seven Charlie Alpha is joining the final approach course."

English is the universal language for every international airport in the world. The controller came back in a British accent. "Good morning UN Seven Charlie Alpha. Cleared to land, runway one-six."

C.T. squeaked the tires on the centerline and taxied off the runway. A ground controller came on frequency. "UN Seven Charlie Alpha, taxi to parking."

The copilot keyed his mic. "This is our first U.N. flight into Baghdad. Could you give us directions?"

"No problem. Take Bravo one to Delta three. The six spots next to the hangar are reserved for United Nations aircraft."

C.T. parked the Gulfstream next to the only other airplane with a UN logo, which he recognized as one of the Embraer 135s he had seen inside the hangar in Amman. By the time the engines spooled down and the stairway was deployed, an immigration officer with a thick moustache and a large badge was waiting on the tarmac.

Coop and Zoe descended the steps to the blacktop. Coop smiled at the agent. "Good morning, sir," he said.

The officer responded in broken English. "You are with the Nations United?"

"Yes," Coop said. "We are with the United Nations." He handed their passports to the man. "We're here from Canada."

The agent looked at the documents and belched, but didn't bother to excuse himself. "How long you will be in Baghdad?"

"Just a couple days."

He looked at Zoe and lifted his eyebrows. "Most UN ladies, they are not...how do say...not handsome. You are a pretty lady."

Zoe placed her hand on top of his. "Well, you're pretty handsome yourself."

The man kissed the top of her hand. "Thank to you for coming to our country. You will let me know if I can be of help. Yes?"

"I certainly will."

The agent stamped their passports and strolled off, but he glanced back once or twice to get another look at Zoe. She waved.

"If we were really married, I think I'd be jealous," Coop said.

Zoe laughed. "If we were really married, you'd have nothing to worry about. He's hardly my type."

They stepped back into the Gulfstream. Coop opened the safe and took out two Glock 23s and four magazines—each holding thirteen rounds. He handed one to Zoe and they both put on belt holsters under loose-fitting shirts and slipped the pistols inside. Before he closed the safe, Coop removed the folder he had taken from the Cyprus Exports' files and he placed it into his briefcase along with the ninety-six thousand dollars already there. He took Moishe's note from his pocket and dialed in the cell phone number.

A man answered. "Yes?"

"Moses sent us. We're at the Baghdad airport, United Nations hangar."

"Wait for a black Mercedes."

Thirty-three

McNamara checked for messages at the hotel's front desk. There was only one. *Director Dutton wants a call immediately.* He shoved it into his pocket and started for the elevator. The lobby was cleaned once a day, usually in the middle of the night when most of the guests were asleep. It was two-thirty in the morning and a maid was vacuuming the lobby carpet around two guys who kept dropping ashes on it as they smoked cigarettes and read newspapers.

Mac approached them. "What's new at the institute?" he said.

The men took their heads out of the sports sections and the older one stared at Mac. "What do you know about the institute?"

"I know it's what you Mossad guys like to call your agency. How long have you been waiting for me?"

"All fuckin' night," the younger one said.

"Gosh, I'm sorry. I should have called your mother and told her you'd be late."

The older guy stood. "Listen motherfucker, this is our country not yours, so watch your mouth or..."

"Or what? Maybe call Director Halevi and tell him what incompetents you are? I could have picked you out from a hundred yards away."

"Fuck you," the young guy said. They folded their newspapers and walked out.

Mac went to his room and ran a bath. He selected a miniature Irish whiskey from the minibar and settled in under the hot water. He was sure he knew what Dutton wanted...has he found Coop yet and when will he be getting him home? Dutton had no idea Zoe was even in the mix.

He did a little math. Tel Aviv was seven hours ahead of D.C., so it was seven-thirty in the evening back there. He'd wait until tomorrow afternoon and reach Director Dutton when he arrived in the morning. He grabbed a towel, finished off the whiskey and pondered what he would actually tell him.

Thirty-four

C.T. did a walk-around of the Gulfstream and then joined Coop and Zoe, who were sitting on a bench waiting for their ride. "The speed tape is working really well. The letters haven't moved."

"That's great," Coop said. "Hey, where will you guys sleep while we're gone?"

"There's a little dorm for visiting pilots and crews. We'll hang out there."

"Okay, keep that pager on twenty-four seven."

"Will do, just don't get yourselves killed. I don't want to go home with an empty airplane."

"We'll try our best."

An electric gate next to the tarmac slid open and a big Mercedes GL550 drove in and pulled to a stop near the Gulfstream. A driver, wearing a chauffeur's hat and jacket, stepped out and opened the rear doors. Coop and Zoe waved goodbye to C.T. and disappeared into the back seats.

On the ride into town, Coop noticed only one thing had changed since they left Baghdad two years ago. The American occupation was over and the only uniforms in sight belonged to the

Iraqi military. A few of the buildings destroyed in the war had been rebuilt, but most were still burned-out shells. The odor coming off the Tigris River hadn't improved either. The smell of pollution was stronger than ever. Coop closed the window.

The driver left the old war zone behind and entered an upscale part of the city. Zoe turned to Coop. "Does this neighborhood look familiar to you?"

Two years ago, when Coop and Zoe had to flee Baghdad, they had contacted a wealthy facilitator who, for a fee, arranged their escape from Iraq. Coop spotted a gated property up ahead. "Mr. Kasim Farzad," Coop said.

Zoe nodded. "You got it."

The driver pulled next to a brass box and tapped in a code. The wrought iron gates creaked as they swung open and the Mercedes drove through onto a circular drive that led to a stately mansion.

As they approached the house, a man dressed in an Arab-style robe stepped out to meet them. "Mr. Farzad is expecting you," he said. Coop and Zoe followed him into the house. Coop was amazed these homes still existed. It was opulent with its high ceilings, marble floors and gold leaf crown mouldings.

Their guide led them to the same large study where they had first met this extraordinary man. "Please make yourselves comfortable. Mr. Farzad will join you shortly." He bowed and left. Coop and Zoe settled into red velvet armchairs and looked around the room. Just as it was when they were last here, it was perfectly appointed. The only out of place item was a security camera mounted in a corner of the ceiling.

Zoe looked at Coop. "Déjà vu?"

"Yeah, all over again."

The double doors opened and a tall, handsome man dressed in suit and tie stepped into the room. He thrust out his hand. "Mr. Cooper, Ms. Fields, we meet again. Welcome."

Coop and Zoe stood and each shook hands with their host. "Thank you," Coop said.

Farzad motioned for them to sit and took a nearby chair for himself. "So, what in the name of God has brought you back to Baghdad?"

"I think Moses told you that we need to get to Iran."

Farzad nodded. "He did, but his communique was brief. Frankly, I did not believe anyone would really want to get into Iran. Most people wish to get out."

"Well, we want to do both. Can you make that happen?"

"Of course I can, but why?"

"We're chasing the paper trail of a wire transfer and for now it leads to Tehran."

Farzad rubbed his chin. "It must be a very important transfer for you to risk your lives for it."

"It is. Our futures depend on our finding it."

"I see, but do either of you speak Farsi?"

Coop looked at Zoe. "Don't look at me. I barely got a 'C' in English," she said.

"What do you suggest?" Coop asked.

Farzad stepped to an antique cabinet and withdrew a bottle and three snifters. "As I recall, you enjoyed this beverage the last time you were here. Let us enjoy a drink while I contemplate this problem."

The three of them listened to the sound of the grandfather clock's pendulum as it echoed off the high ceiling. After what seemed like hours to Coop and Zoe, but was only thirty-five minutes on the clock, Farzad spoke. "How much did Moses say I would charge to get you in and out of Iran?"

"Twenty-five thousand each way," Coop said.

"Very well. I shall go with you. I speak impeccable Farsi."

Coop was taken aback. From what he knew of Farzad, he was a guy who pulled strings to make things happen, but wasn't one to risk his own safety along the way. "That's very generous of you, but I don't think we can afford your personal services."

"You have to understand something, Mr. Cooper. I despise Iran. Not the Iranian people, but the Iranian government. Whenever I have an opportunity to put a stick in the eye of that regime, I do it. My additional fee to guide you is zero."

"Are you sure?" Coop said.

Farzad grinned. "I am quite sure, Mr. Cooper. Now, while we drink, let me tell you the plan I have devised."

Thirty-five

McNamara dialed the number for Director Dutton and it was answered by his secretary on the first ring. "Lorraine, this is Agent McNamara. I'm returning Director Dutton's call."

"Oh, thank goodness, he's been waiting to hear from you. Hang on while I switch you through."

"Remind him to engage his scrambler."

Mac waited on hold while a recording by Enya whispered new-age music into his ear. After a minute or two, Dutton came on. "McNamara, what the hell is going on over there? I told you to keep me in the loop."

"Is your scrambler on, sir?" Mac asked.

"Yes, it's on. Fill me in."

"Okay, I found Coop, but he has someone with him."

"Someone? Who?"

"Zoe Fields."

"I don't get it. She sent in her resignation two years ago, right after the Iraq operation. Why is she with Cooper?"

McNamara hesitated before answering. How he phrased his answer could determine Coop and Zoe's future. "It seems Zoe's domestic partner is a bigwig at Swiss Commerce Bank in Zurich and Zoe engaged her help to recover the nine million dollars that disappeared during the Iraq operation."

"Are you saying that money actually exists? I thought it was only urban legend here at the Agency."

"Yeah, it exists and Zoe found it. But she didn't think it would look good for the Agency if out of the blue an ex-agent wired the Agency nine million dollars. So, your old buddy, Mizrahi, agreed to have it sent through him."

Dutton was never well known for having an overabundance of patience. "Get to the point, for God's sake."

"Okay, the money never arrived in Israel. Zoe was angry and began searching for it, but all of a sudden, she dropped off everyone's radar. Coop went to Israel to find her and he did—in Mizrahi's office. A few minutes later, Mizrahi was murdered. Now Coop and Zoe are fugitives in Israel."

"Well, get them both the fuck back here."

McNamara took his time again. "I would, but there's a problem."

"Goddammit, McNamara, spit it out."

"They're on their way to Iran to look for the money."

"Jesus H. Christ. If Iran gets ahold of them, it'll create an international incident. The whole fuckin' Middle East could explode. Can you stop them?"

"You know Coop. When he gets a head of steam, there's no stopping him. Look, he knows this op isn't sanctioned by the Agency and he knows if it goes south the Agency can't back him. He's ready to take the fall if he gets caught."

Dutton let out a deep sigh. "Okay, but if something big happens, let me know before the rest of the world finds out about it."

~ * ~

Rachel Kagan stepped into the reception room and approached the secretary. "Director Halevi asked that I stop by."

The secretary pushed an intercom button and let the Director know that Rachel was waiting. He requested she be shown in immediately.

Halevi greeted her with a kiss to both cheeks. "Rachel, Rachel, the prettiest agent in the institute." He patted a chair cushion. "Please, sit for a cup of tea."

After filling two cups, Halevi said, "Rachel, tell me we are close to finding Cooper and Fields."

"I'd like to tell you that, sir, but we aren't."

"Are they still in Israel?"

"As far as we can tell, yes."

"And why are you so sure of this?"

"Because their Agency contact, that guy McNamara, is still hanging around. If he had gotten them out, he'd be gone too."

Halevi nodded. "I don't have to tell you that if another government gives them asylum, it will create an international incident. The entire Middle East could be shaken."

"I understand, sir."

Halevi stood and started for the door. "Please, if they escape, let me know before the rest of the world finds out about it."

Thirty-six

Farzad refilled everyone's glasses, then took a healthy gulp and leaned in with his hands folded. "First you have to understand that if we get caught, we will be jailed for a long time. I'm sure you have read about those three American hikers who accidentally wandered into Iran last year and were accused of being spies. They were sentenced to eight years in prison."

"We've worked for the Agency for over twenty-five years. We know the risks," Coop said.

"Very good. Then, from now on you are a wealthy, conservative Iranian businessman. Ms. Fields is your wife and I am your chauffeur and spokesman should anyone wish to speak with you."

"What about papers?" Zoe asked.

"That is the easiest part; I employ an artist on my payroll. He will use your old photos and have the new passports made in two hours." Farzad pushed a key on the intercom and gave a command in Arabic. He looked back at Coop and Zoe. "My tailor will be here in five minutes to fit your clothes. Now, if you will excuse me, I have arrangements to make for our trip."

"Mr. Farzad," Coop said. "I haven't paid you." He snapped open his briefcase and removed twenty bundles of hundred-dollar bills.

Farzad didn't bother to count them, just scooped them up and headed for the door. "I will be back in a few hours."

Coop and Zoe looked at each other like they had just won the lottery. "Am I dreaming?" Coop said.

"Let's just hope it's not a nightmare," Zoe answered.

A light knock came on the door and it was opened without waiting for a response. A tiny man with a close-cropped gray beard and spectacles worn low on his nose stepped into the room. "Good afternoon," he said in perfect English. "I am Yasir, Mr. Farzad's clothes maker."

Yasir took Zoe's measurements first and then worked on Coop. When he had all his notes made, he said, "One hour, please. I will have your garments ready for you."

The butler brought a tray of snacks along with a steaming pot and set it on a table in the corner of the room. Zoe checked it out. "Looks good," she said.

Coop said he wasn't hungry but asked, "What is it?"

"Well, there's freshly baked flat bread and a bowl of hummus and there's an assortment of dried fruits...looks like pears and apricots."

"I could go for a cup of coffee. Is there some in that pot?"

Zoe lifted the lid, dunked her finger inside and licked it. "It's mint tea—delicious."

Coop wrinkled his nose. "I hate tea."

Zoe poured herself a cup. "Suit yourself," she said.

Coop relented and picked at the food, but he wouldn't taste the tea. Before the tray was empty, Yasir knocked on the door and re-entered the study. He handed each of them a pile of neatly ironed garments and pointed to a door. "There is a day room. You may change in there."

Zoe went first. When she returned, her head was covered in a black veil with only an opening for her eyes. The rest of her body, head to foot, was covered by a loose black garment.

"Quite stylish for a burka," Coop said.

Yasir interrupted. "This is not really a burka. A burka also covers the eyes. This is a niqab over her head and an abaya over her body; they are very common for women in Iran."

Coop picked up his pile of clothes and took his turn in the adjacent room. He emerged wearing a collarless white shirt, white trousers and a long white cloak secured around the middle by a cummerbund.

Yasir reached into a case and came out with a brimless, short, rounded cap. He placed it on Coop's head. "This is a kufi cap. Many men wear these in Iran."

The door opened and Farzad stepped into the room. 'Well, well, now you look like Mr. Daryush Jafari and his wife Kamraneh." He handed each of them a passport. "So, tell me again, exactly why we are risking our lives to go to Iran."

They took seats around the coffee table and Coop opened his briefcase. He took out the manila folder he had confiscated from Nikolas back in Cyprus and removed three sheets of computer-printed paper. He handed them to Farzad.

"Okay, you'll see on the first page that a guy named Nikolas Georgiou, who works for Cyprus Exports, took in a wire transfer from Zurich for nine million dollars. Zoe was the one who sent that money. Georgiou was supposed to redirect it to the Israeli Mossad director, Abraham Mizrahi, but if you look on page two, you'll see he sent it instead to Iran. Page three is the receipt confirmation sent back to Nikolas from the City of Tehran's Office of Accounting. It's signed by a guy named Kamran Rashidi. We have to find that guy to find out where the money went from there."

"I understand," Farzad said. He looked at his watch. "It is now a little after two o'clock. The drive will take us eleven hours and I prefer to make it at night, so my butler will show you to rooms where you may nap until we leave at nine o'clock this evening."

Thirty-seven

The butler knocked on each of their doors at eight-thirty. Coop put on his white pants and strapped on his holster and Glock. He pulled the white collarless shirt over his head and left it untucked to cover his waist. In one hand he carried his briefcase and in the other he carried a shopping bag containing his white cloak, cummerbund and Kufi cap.

Zoe put on a pair of Levi's and hooked up her holster and pistol, then pulled on a large tee shirt to cover them. She tucked her black abaya and the black niqab head covering under her arm and joined Coop at the elevator.

Coop pushed the button marked LL and when the elevator doors opened, they stepped into a large garage that housed about a dozen vehicles. Parked in the center was a black limousine which several of Farzad's assistants were busy loading with food and other supplies. Farzad saw Coop and Zoe and motioned them to join him. "You are well rested?" he said.

Coop gave a thumbs up. "Yes, thanks for the accommodations." He pointed at the car. "Quite a rig. I have to say I didn't expect this."

"You and your wife are important people who garner respect. In Iran, officials and military are very careful not to upset important people. Let me show you the vehicle." He patted the roof like a proud father would to the head of his scholarly son. "I am quite excited; I do not get to drive this often. It is the flagship of my fleet. An armored Mercedes Benz S600 Pullman Guard, equipped with bulletproof metal and glass along with dry running tires."

Coop lifted his brows. "I'm curious what something like this sets you back."

Farzad smiled. "You know the saying, Mr. Cooper. If you have to ask the price, you cannot afford it." He pointed to the front of the vehicle. "Come, I will show you the power plant." The hood was open and one of the assistants was checking the fluids in the engine. Farzad pointed to it. "This is a twin turbocharged V12. It accelerates eight thousand pounds of metal from zero to sixty miles per hour in eight point six seconds."

Zoe looked at Coop. "Please don't ask what kind of gas mileage it gets."

The assistants closed the hood and the trunk and stepped away from the limo. Farzad opened one of the rear doors and held out his hand. "Mr. Jafari, Mrs. Jafari, the passenger compartment is all yours."

Coop looked inside. Facing forward were two leather arm chair seats separated by a console, and facing backward were two more of the same. They both took the forward-facing ones, so they could communicate with Farzad while the plexiglass partition was retracted.

Farzad tossed a chauffeur's cap and jacket on the passenger side and took his place in the driver's seat. He turned around and handed Zoe a piece of paper. "These are four basic Farsi words. You have two hours to memorize them." He fired up the engine and peeled rubber as he accelerated through the open garage doors.

Twenty minutes after leaving the residence, a road sign written in Arabic denoting a four-lane highway appeared. Farzad headed up the ramp and as soon as he joined the road going northeast, he took over the left lane and accelerated the behemoth to 130 k.p.h. Coop leaned back and closed his eyes. For now, the sounds and smells of the Middle East had disappeared.

Zoe glanced over at Coop. He looked so peaceful she hated to rouse him, but she knew she had to. She poked him with her elbow. "Should we start memorizing Farsi?"

Coop opened his eyes. "I guess we better."

Zoe handed him the paper. It read: *YES= bal, NO= ne, Please= khahesh, Thank you= mam'noon.*

They both began pronouncing the words out loud. Farzad heard them and said, "please, you are butchering the language. Pronounce after me." For the next hour he said the words and Coop and Zoe repeated them.

The obvious suddenly occurred to Coop. "Hold it," he said. "How can we answer a question asked to us in Farsi if we don't understand it?"

Farzad laughed. "I wondered how long it would take for you to come to that realization. Signals," he said.

"Okay, what're the signals?"

"I touch my right ear and you answer yes, I mean bal. I touch my left ear and you answer ne. I touch my nose and it's kahesh, I touch my chin and it's mam'noon."

Farzad looked at his watch. "The border is less than an hour away. There is a little mountain village about twenty minutes from here. We will use the facilities and put on our clothes there." His estimate was accurate and they pulled into a fuel station at eleven-thirty.

Coop and Zoe went into the bathrooms clutching their bundles of clothes. When they came out, Zoe was covered in black with only her eyes showing and Coop was dressed in white from head to toe. They slipped back into the passenger compartment and waited for Farzad, who joined them five minutes later. He was already wearing blue slacks and a white shirt, so when he slipped on his blue jacket and blue cap, he fit the image of a well-dressed chauffeur to a tee. He turned to get a peek at Coop and Zoe. "Ms. Fields, you look so nice, perhaps I'll let you keep the outfit," he said.

"Kahesh, ne," Zoe said. They all broke out laughing.

Leaving Iraq was no problem. Farzad stepped out of the limo and spoke briefly with the border guard, who smiled widely when Farzad handed him a large bottle of El Massaya Arak.

There was a quarter of a mile separation between the Iraq border agents and the Iranian ones. As soon as the limo was out of sight of the Iraqis, Farzad pulled to the side of the road, opened the glove compartment and took out a screwdriver and two license plates. "I will be about five minutes," he said.

He hustled to the front and then to the back of the limo, removed the Iraq plates and replaced them with Iranian ones, then he jumped back into the driver's seat. "We are Iranians now," he said, as he pushed the button to close the plexiglass partition between them.

There were two guards inside the Iran border kiosk, but only one came out. The other was stuffing his mouth with food from a lunch pail. Farzad stepped out of the car and handed him three passports—all the work of his counterfeiter—and waited patiently while the agent examined them.

The guard pointed to the back seat and said something in Farsi. Farzad nodded and stuck his head inside the limo, retracted the partition to the passenger compartment and whispered, "signals." He then pushed a button to open the rear smoked glass window that faced the guard. The uniformed man looked inside. Farzad stood behind him.

Three or four sentences spoken in Farsi came at Coop and Zoe. The only thing they understood was the name Jafari. Farzad touched his right ear. "Bal," Coop said. The man said something else and thrust out his hand. Farzad rubbed his chin. Coop shook the man's hand and said, "mam'noon."

The agent was beaming when Farzad gave him a bottle of El Massaya. He handed the passports back and returned to the kiosk. Farzad joined Coop and Zoe in the limo. "So, what was the conversation I had?" Coop asked.

"The officer asked if you were having a nice trip and you said yes. Then he said it is a pleasure to meet you, Mr. Jafari, and you said thank you. Farsi is an easy language, is it not?"

There was a third quarter moon in the sky that lit most of the mountainous terrain, which the huge Mercedes was negotiating flawlessly with Farzad at the wheel. Coop glanced at the digital clock built into the console. It was two-twenty. He leaned forward toward the open partition. "Do you need any help driving?" Coop asked.

Farzad waved his hand. "No, I am fine, but if you could open the small refrigerator and hand me an iced tea, that would be nice."

Coop handed the drink to Farzad. "What time do you think we'll get there?"

"The mountains have slowed us up a bit, but in a few miles, we will hit the central desert plateau and I will step harder on the accelerator. The speed limit is a hundred and twenty."

"Miles per hour?"

Farzad laughed. "No, kilometers per hour. That is about seventy-five in miles. I would say we should be in Tehran by seven-thirty."

"Any idea what time the government offices open there?"

"If my memory serves me correctly, they open at eight in the morning and close at two in the afternoon."

"Perfect. Hey, Zoe's asleep, I'm going to join her, if that's okay with you."

"By all means. Get some rest, tomorrow could be a big day."

Coop reclined his seat and drifted off to sleep. He dreamt of sitting behind the bench at Josh's basketball game and cheering wildly when Josh stole the ball and went in for a layup. The ball hung on the rim, but before he could see if it dropped into the basket, that dream disappeared and was replaced by another where he was in a prison cell. He was looking through the bars into the yard, where gallows were being erected. A hangman, carrying a basketball, entered his cell. He woke with a start.

Zoe was already awake. "Man, that must have been some kind of dream. You were trying to yell, but nothing came out," she said.

Coop rubbed his eyes. "Yeah, I'm used to them. I could go for a cup of coffee."

"You got it." She opened a teak cabinet and pushed a button marked with the outline of a mug. When it was filled, she handed the cup to Coop. "Black, just how you like it."

Farzad smelled the coffee and leaned toward the compartment "I would love one of those."

"No problem," Zoe said. She tapped the machine again.

Coop looked through the smoked glass window. "The sun's coming up," he said. "Hey, Mr. Chauffeur, are we close?"

Farzad looked at the clock. "Right on time."

The limo joined the heavy early morning traffic outside Tehran and when the sign for the City Centre appeared, Farzad took the exit and navigated to the Tehran government building on Khomeini Square. He parked behind two other limos in a zone that was designated in Farsi letters: For Government Officers Only "There are pitas in the refrigerator," he said.

Mr. and Mrs. Jafari and their chauffeur had breakfast while they waited for the Tehran Office of Accounting to open.

Thirty-eight

They wolfed down their breakfast in less than ten minutes. Coop looked at the clock; it was five minutes to eight and dozens of employees were scurrying to get inside the government building before the opening bell.

"Any idea what our guy looks like?" Farzad asked.

"Not a clue," Coop said.

"How do you want me to play this?"

"If it's all right with you, I'd like you to go inside and ask to see Kamran Rashidi. Try to get him in a private setting and tell him he has come to the attention of a very important man, who would like to offer him employment in the private sector. By the way, what's a good yearly salary in this country?"

Farzad thought for a minute. "I would say the equivalent of twenty-five thousand U.S. dollars."

"Great, tell him the starting salary is equal to ninety-six thousand dollars. Tell him your employer is waiting in the limousine to talk with him."

Farzad waited twenty minutes, just in case the guy was a tardy employee. He tucked in his shirt, put on his cap and turned around.

"I am putting up the partition. No one will be able to see through it or the smoked windows. If anyone comes snooping around, just pretend the limo is empty. No one in his right mind would be upset with this vehicle being parked in a VIP zone."

He got out and locked the doors.

The City of Tehran Office of Accounting was located on the fifth floor of the twelve-floor building. Farzad stepped from the elevator and approached a very beautiful olive-skinned woman wearing a scarf that was draped over the top of her head and below her chin. He handed her a phony business card printed in Farsi and using the title of respect in Iran, asked to see Âghâ Rashidi.

Apparently Rashidi wasn't a very busy man; Farzad only waited five minutes before being escorted into his office. When Farzad was young, he had wanted to be an actor, but his parents wouldn't hear of it. They would have been proud of his performance this morning. Within the first three minutes, he had the hook set and a minute later he was reeling Rashidi in. The young man was beaming and asked when he could meet Âghâ Jafari, this mysterious employer.

Coop and Zoe had their eyes fixed on the building's front doors. When a perfectly dressed chauffeur and a poorly dressed young man walked out, Coop grinned ear to ear. "Here we go," he said.

Farzad clicked the locks and opened a rear door for Rashidi. When the young man stared inside at the presence of a wealthy well-dressed man and a perfectly covered woman, his pulse went into overdrive. He extended his hand and spewed out a sentence with the name Jafari in it.

Coop recognized the surname. He shook Rashidi's hand and said, "mam'noon," then patted the seat across from him.

Kamran Rashidi stepped into the limo and sank into the soft leather seat. Farzad closed the doors and clicked the locks. Coop and Zoe took their pistols from under their gowns and pointed them directly at the young man.

His natural tan complexion turned to a shade of alabaster and he rattled off a couple Farsi sentences. "Do you speak English?" Coop asked.

"English? Ye...yes, sir."

"Very good," Coop said. "Do you mind if we search for a weapon?" Before Rashidi could answer, Zoe was patting him down. She gave Coop a thumbs up.

Coop and Zoe lifted their gowns and replaced their pistols into their holsters. "Something to drink?" Coop asked.

"Water ple...please."

Zoe popped the top from a bottle and handed it to Kamran. He took it from her, but try as he may he couldn't steady his hand long enough to drink it. "We want to know about a wire transfer from Cyprus Exports to your accounting office. It was for nine million U.S. dollars. By any chance, do you remember it?" she asked.

Sweat dripped down the sides of Rashadi's face and a drop hung from the tip of his nose. "I, I...yes, I remember it." He made another attempt at the water and spilled most of it on his lap. "Khahesh, khahesh...please, please, I'll give you the money back."

"The nine million?" Coop said.

Rashidi eyes were damp and when he opened them wide, a couple tears dripped out. "The nine million? I...I did what you told me to do. I wired it off to a new location. I'm talking about the two-hundred and fifty thousand dollars your man gave to me."

"Who gave you the two-fifty?" Zoe said.

"Your man. He opened a case and it was filled with dollars. He said I could keep it if I sent on that wire transfer."

Coop took out the same photo he had showed Nikolas in Cyprus. It was the one of Joseph Halevi that appeared in the paper when he was appointed Mossad director. "Is this the man who carried the briefcase?"

Rashidi squinted as he looked at it. "No, I think this man is older."

"Where did you send the nine million?" Coop said.

"I...I don't really remember."

Coop lifted his gown and removed his Glock from its holster. He put it between Kamran Rashidi's eyes. "You're a fuckin' liar."

"No, it is the truth. I don't remember, but...but I have a record of it."

"A record? Where? Where is this record?"

"I buried it in the dead files."

"What are dead files?'

"They are transactions that took place at least twenty years ago."

Coop put the pistol away and put his hand on Kamran's shoulder. "Son, you don't look like a guy who would be a bean counter for the government. Are you happy here in Iran?"

Kamran looked down at his shoes. "No, sir. My father is a tyrant."

Coop noticed a cut above Kamran's eye. He pointed to it. "Did he do that?"

"He was beating my mother and I tried to stop him. I hate that bastard."

"Maybe you have dreamed of a life somewhere else?" Coop said.

He began to sob. "Yes, sir, I have."

Zoe moved next to Rashidi and cradled his body next to hers. "Kamran, let us help you."

Between gasps he said, "Why, why would you do that?"

"Because if you help us, we'll help you."

"How?"

"You go back into your office and get that record from the dead files. Then, we'll drive you to your home. You pick up your case full of money and passport, pack a bag and say goodbye to your mother. We'll get you out of Iran and fly you to another country. With all that money, you can start a new life."

"Do you mean I can keep the money?"

"And start a new life," Zoe said.

The young man began to sob again. "But I don't know anyone n another country. Where will I live?"

Coop lifted Kamran's head to make direct eye contact. "Don't worry, I know a guy your age who happens to be looking for a roommate. I think the two of you will have a lot in common."

Zoe rubbed her hand up and down the young man's back. "Come on, Kamran, what d'ya say?"

Farzad unlocked the doors and Kamran jumped out and headed back into the office building. Farzad looked at Coop. "What s the chance he spills the beans?"

"You never know in this business, but I'm betting he'll go through with it."

Zoe added her opinion. "I think so too, but just in case, you'd better start this beast and have it ready for a quick getaway."

Five minutes passed; another ten minutes passed...thirty; forty-five. "I'm glad I didn't bet," Coop said.

Just before an hour elapsed, Kamran came hustling through the front door of the building. His hands were empty. Farzad stepped out of the car and held the rear door open for the young man. He scooted inside and Farzad hit the locks, jumped into the driver's seat and took off.

"Do you have it?" Coop asked.

Kamran pulled up his shirt and removed a folder that had been shoved down the front of his trousers. "I have it."

Coop and Zoe huddled together and read the record of three wire transfers. It turned out Kamran was a very thorough junior accountant.

The first document confirmed the receipt of nine million dollars, sent by Zoe Fields to Cyprus Exports. The second document verified that Cyprus Exports then sent the money to the Tehran Office of Accounting. The final document, bearing the official seal of the City of Tehran, was the receipt for routing nine million dollars from the Office of Accounting to a discreet numbered account at the Luxembourg Bank of Trade in Luxembourg.

"What was the number of the account?" Coop asked.

Kamran shrugged. "We were never allowed to keep a record of any numbered account, so I didn't." Coop's eyes narrowed.

"I swear. I don't have the number."

Coop dropped the file into his briefcase and turned to Kamran. "You did a good job. Now, give the chauffeur your address and we'll get you out of here."

Thirty-nine

The limo looked out of place in the middle-class neighborhood where Kamran lived with his parents. Farzad opened the door for him. He was as white as a sheet. "Do you need one of us to go with you?" Farzad asked.

"Could you come? I'm a little afraid of those other people."

"I would be happy to." Farzad looked at Coop and Coop nodded.

The Rashidi home was on the top floor of what in America would be called a duplex. Kamran led the way up the stairs and Farzad followed. He took a seat in the entry hall and Kamran went to the back of the house to get his things and bid his farewell.

The house was quiet until the silence was broken by the wailing of a woman. Farzad knew Kamran must be talking to his mother. Another minute later, he heard a man's voice yelling over the top of the cries. "Uh, oh," he murmured.

The last thing Farzad wanted was to interfere in the family argument, but that was why Kamran had asked him to be there. He walked down the hall and stepped into the room at the same instant that Kamran's father slapped his son across the face. In Farsi, Farzad said, "that's enough. Your son is leaving with us."

The senior Rashidi looked at him with crazed eyes and ran from the room. Farzad turned to Kamran. "Do you have your things?"

Kamran picked up a duffel and a briefcase. "Yes." He went to the sobbing woman and hugged her. "Goodbye, Mother."

Farzad and Kamran started down the hallway. A tremendous blast came from behind and shotgun pellets sprayed holes in the ceiling. "Stop," the older man yelled in his Farsi tongue.

Coop and Zoe heard the gunshot. "Zoe, get in the driver's seat. I'm going inside," Coop said.

He pulled out his pistol, raced up the stairs and flung the door open. Farzad and Kamran were frozen in their positions, listening to the old man rant and rave, while he waved his gun in their direction.

Kamran's father was taken aback by the sight of an aristocrat holding a gun and he lowered his weapon. Coop approached him and pointed his Glock at the man's head. "Farzad, tell him what's going to happen if he tries to stop this."

Farzad translated and Coop relieved the man of his shotgun. "Okay, let's go," Coop said. The three men scrambled down the stairs and into the limo. Zoe stepped on the accelerator and they sped off.

Zoe stayed at the wheel until they were out of the neighborhood before switching seats with Farzad. She sat next to Kamran and quietly spoke to him trying to help him validate his decision.

Coop noticed as they left the city, they were headed due west on a route that was different from the one on which they had come in. "Charting a new course, Captain?" he asked.

Farzad leaned his head toward the back seats. "Very soon the RAHVAR will be looking on the highways for us and this is a hard vehicle to miss. I am taking a smaller road through the mountains."

"I'm guessing RAVAR is Iran's highway patrol."

The limo took a hard right and Farzad stepped up the speed. "Yes, and they are very good at what they do."

It took less than an hour before the road became narrow— barely wide enough for cars to pass each other. It was the initial climb into the mountains, but it didn't deter Farzad. He kept up his speed as he weaved his way around the curves. Kamran wasn't used to this type of driving; after another two hours his face color had changed again. This time it was a combination of gray and green.

Zoe leaned her head through the partition opening. "Mr. Farzad, you better stop for a minute. Kamran is going to puke."

"There is a fueling station two miles ahead. We will take a break there."

Farzad arranged for the tank to be filled, then joined Coop and Zoe for a quick snack from the refrigerator. Kamran was in the bathroom doing what had to be done. "Can we get out of these clothes?" Coop asked Farzad.

"I do not think that would be a good idea yet. Who knows what we will encounter in the next few hours?"

"How long to the border?" Zoe said.

"We are going to come up on a small plateau where we will make up some time. I would guess about five hours."

Kamran came out of the bathroom looking a couple shades healthier than when he went in. The four of them piled back into the limo and Farzad sped around the last few miles of curves before they reached the plateau. Once the road straightened out, he accelerated the big black beast to a hundred and five miles an hour. The next three hours were uneventful and all the passengers fell asleep.

Coop had the same dream. Josh put the ball on the rim, but before it dropped into the basket, a hangman carrying a basketball appeared. Coop woke abruptly and wiped the sweat from his forehead.

The sun had set while Coop slept and now the only outside light came from the high-beams emitted from the Mercedes' xenon headlights. The plateau ended and they were back in the mountains, navigating a one-lane road next to a sheer cliff. Farzad made a hairpin turn and screeched to a stop. The limo's headlights lit up a white SUV with the black letters RAHVAR printed across its doors. It was blocking the road.

Zoe and Kamran woke with a start. "What is it?" Zoe asked.

Farzad pointed ahead. "National police."

Two uniformed officers, both carrying LED flashlights and automatic rifles stepped from the SUV and approached the limo's driver door. One of them directed his light at the window and yelled something in Farsi. "They are ordering us to get out," Farzad said.

Coop turned to Kamran. "You're going to have to tell them you're not being kidnapped. Tell them we're your friends and it's your choice, not your father's, to be with us. Can you do that?"

Kamran's mouth was so dry he could barely swallow. "I...I think I can."

Coop patted him on the back. "I know you can."

Zoe put her niqab back over her head and Coop buttoned his robe and put on his kufi cap. Farzad donned his chauffeur's hat and the four occupants stepped out of the limo.

The officer in charge approached Kamran, shined his light onto his face and barked out a question. Kamran gave the answer Coop had instructed him to give. The officer smacked him twice across the face with the back of his hand.

Farzad stepped forward and began speaking in Farsi. Coop and Zoe assumed he was making a case to support Kamran's statement, but the officer wasn't interested in listening. He took the butt of his gun and whipped it across Farzad's left cheek, snapping his head backwards. A three-inch slice of skin split open like a watermelon and blood came gushing down the side of his face, changing the color of his shirt from plain white to bright red.

The aggressive officer turned his attention to Coop and Zoe and began yelling at them in Farsi. They had no idea what he was saying and both stayed mute. He raised his weapon, motioned for his assistant to do the same and approached them.

Instinctively, Coop and Zoe placed their hands under their robes and slipped their pistols from their holsters. When the policemen were close enough to smell the garlic on their breath, Coop and Zoe fired. The officers' faces had looks of surprise as they crumpled to the ground.

Coop grabbed one of their flashlights and inspected Farzad's wound. "We have to close that up," he said.

Zoe started for the limo. "I'll get the first aid kit." She returned and began bathing Farzad's wound in hydrogen peroxide, but the blood continued to pour out.

"Put pressure on it," Coop said. He ran back to the car to get his briefcase. Inside it, he still had two bundles of cash that were being held together with paper clamps. He opened the clamps, let the money spill all over the bottom of the case and hurried back to Farzad.

Zoe had the wound clean and was pushing hard against it with a wad of gauze from the first aid kit. "Let go of the top half," Coop said. Zoe pulled the gauze away and Coop quickly clamped the two sides of skin together. "Now, the bottom," Coop said. Zoe let go and Coop clamped the rest of the wound.

"How bad is the pain?" Coop asked Farzad.

"It is pretty bad,"

"Okay, Zoe's going to drive and you'll get in the back with Kamran and me. We'll take turns putting ice from the fridge on that cheek."

Zoe helped Farzad into the back seat, while Coop directed Kamran to help him get the two dead policemen into the SUV. When that task was completed, Coop started the car, put it in gear and let it drive itself off the steep cliff. Zoe fired up the limo's engine and they headed for Iraq.

The entire right side of Farzad's face was swollen and turning purple. "How are you holding up?" Coop said.

"I will make it. Do not worry."

"Where are we?" Coop asked.

"We are about one hundred miles from the border. When we cross, we will be in the Kurdish region of Iraq. The first city we will come to is Sulaymaniyah and they have a good-sized airport. Can you get your plane up there?"

"Yeah, if I could call for it."

Farzad pointed to a cabinet. "There is a satellite phone in there."

Coop opened the cabinet and checked out the phone. It was cradled in a charger and a green light was blinking. He knew C.T.'s number by memory and punched it in. When it was answered, he pushed nine to bypass the pager. "Coop, is that you?" C.T. said.

"Yeah, listen up. I need you to get the Gulfstream to a place called Sulaymaniyah. It's about a hundred and fifty miles north of Baghdad. Meet us there in two hours."

Coop looked back at Farzad. "Okay, now, how do we get across the border?"

~ * ~

The limo's headlights illuminated a sign designating the upcoming border between Iran and Iraq. Zoe pulled to the side of the road. Coop grabbed the Iraq license plates and the screwdriver from the glove compartment and ran around the limo exchanging them for the Iran ones.

The road approaching the border was straight, wide and flat. Zoe turned off the headlights and punched the accelerator to the floor. The limo's speed maxed out at a hundred and twenty-one miles an hour.

The Iranian border guards didn't spot the limo until it was only twenty yards away. They dropped the wooden gate arms and held up their hands to signal a stop, but Zoe kept her foot to the pedal, turned on the high beams and headed straight for them.

When the guards realized, the limo wasn't going to slow down, they took out their automatic weapons and began firing.

The outer layer of armored metal absorbed the bullets and the reinforced glass cracked, but it kept the slugs from entering. Zoe blasted through the gates and kept driving toward the Iraq border crossing.

The Iraqi guards heard the shots and were on high alert when Zoe pulled up at their station. One of the guards caught a look at the shot-up limo and yelled to his partner for help. The two men cautiously approached the vehicle with their sidearms drawn. Coop let down one of the back seat windows and yelled, "Khahesh, khahesh, please, please."

One of the guards snuck up on the window and peered inside. Farzad handed him his authentic Iraq credentials and spoke in Arabic. "I am an official with the Iraq government and have just escaped capture in Iran. I am in need of medical attention. Can you provide us escort to the airport in Sulaymaniyah?

The guards immediately recognized Farzad as an important figure in Iraq. One of them kicked the starter on a motorcycle and flipped on a set of blinking red and blue lights. The other guard handed back the credentials and said, "It was an honor to serve you, Mr. Farzad, sir. God speed."

The motorcycle took off and Zoe fell in behind it.

Forty

The Gulfstream was sitting on the tarmac at the Sulaymaniyah airport when Zoe followed the motorcycle through the gate. She headed straight to the plane and screeched to a stop where C.T. and his copilot were anxiously waiting for them.

Coop jumped out of the back seat, signaled for help and the two pilots came running. Coop motioned toward Farzad. "Help me get him in the plane. Twenty minutes ago, I injected him with some morphine from the medical kit and he's out cold."

C.T. and his copilot each took one of Farzad's arms and hoisted it over their shoulder, then dragged him up the stairs and into the passenger compartment where they laid him out on a reclined seat.

Coop and Zoe had been so focused on Farzad they had neglected Kamran. He was shriveled up and shivering in the corner of one of the limo's back seats. Zoe went to him. His cheeks were bright red from the policeman's blows. "Hey, buddy, are you doing all right?"

"I don't know what I am doing here? I think I want to go home."

Zoe hugged him tight. "Don't worry, Kamran, everything is going to be fine now. In a couple hours you'll be settled in a new country. Trust me, you'll be in a better place."

He held on to her like a scared child. "Are you sure?"

"I'm sure. Now get your stuff and get on the plane."

Coop parked the limo in a nearby lot, but before he locked it, he took the satellite phone and charger with him. When he got back to the Gulfstream, everyone was aboard and the turbines were beginning to wind up. He leaned on the door handle to lock it in place and then made his way to the cockpit.

"What's the plan?" C.T. said.

"Okay, our first stop is Baghdad. We have to get Farzad to a hospital. He's gonna need some plastic work on that cheek."

"Then what?"

"Then we head to Cyprus."

As soon as C.T. leveled off, Coop hooked up the satellite phone and punched in his home number. Fran answered. "Who is this?"

"It's me," Coop said.

"Oh, Coop, I've been worried sick. Is everything all right?"

"Yeah, everything's going good."

"So, that means you've cleared up all the misunderstandings?"

Coop hesitated. "Well, not exactly, but I'm close." Fran didn't respond. "Fran, are you mad?" he said.

"Coop, you know I'm not mad. I'm just disappointed... disappointed for Josh."

"Yeah, I understand. I feel terrible. Is he there?"

"I'll put him on. Get home as soon as you can. Love ya."

Coop tapped his hand nervously on the receiver while he waited for Josh to pick up. "Dad? Is that you?"

"Hi, buddy. How're you doing?"

"I'm doing great. How about you?"

"Oh, I'm just fine. Listen, Josh, I have to apologize...again. I won't be home for your first game."

"I know, Dad, the game was last night."

"Oh, man, I lost track of the days. How did you do?"

"The coach played me as seventh man. I got six points."

Coop could feel his pulse beating in his throat. "That's so great. I'm so proud of you. When's the next game?"

"We're in a holiday tournament three days before Christmas. Do you think, maybe...like, maybe you'll be home for it?"

"I'm not going to make you another promise I can't keep, but I'm going to try my darndest to be there."

"Okay, Dad. I love you."

"Love you too."

By the time C.T. greased the Gulfstream onto the Baghdad runway, Farzad was awake and lucid. Coop gave him a bottle of water. "I can't thank you enough," Coop said.

Farzad took a healthy gulp. "It was my pleasure."

"I owe you more money. Your car is pretty dinged up and it's sitting in Sulaymaniyah."

"You owe me nothing more. I loved the adventure. It made me feel alive again, like I did when I was twenty-five."

An attendant brought a wheelchair to get Farzad from the plane to a taxi. Farzad thrust out his hand and Coop squeezed it. "You're going to have a pretty good scar," Coop said.

"It will be my badge of honor. Until we meet again, my friend, stay well." He gave a weak salute and the attendant pushed him toward the terminal.

C.T. fired up the turbines and taxied out for takeoff. The normal flight time from Baghdad to Larnaca was an hour and forty-five minutes, but there was a westerly flow at twenty-eight thousand feet that pushed the Gulfstream to Cyprus in an hour twenty.

Coop put his hand on Kamran's shoulder. "Ready for a new start?" he said.

Kamran nodded. "I...I think so."

The taxi took them to the front of Cyprus Exports in less than fifteen minutes. Coop asked the driver to hang around and he, Zoe

nd Kamran went inside. Nikolas looked up from the game he was
laying on his iPhone and recognized Coop. "What more do you
vant of me?" he asked.

"Are you still looking for a roommate?"

"Yes...but I can't find one."

Coop held up his palms. "Nikolas Georgiou meet Kamran
Rashidi. You guys are about to be roommates with a half a million
dollars between you. Use it wisely." He and Zoe returned to the
vaiting cab and headed back to the airport.

Coop told C.T. to hang around Larnaca for the next few days
nd told him to let McNamara know he and Zoe would be traveling
vith their Canadian passports back to Tel Aviv on a commercial
light. They landed at Ben Gurion Airport a little after midnight.

Forty-one

McNamara was waiting at the gate when Coop and Zoe stepped off the jetway. He made eye contact, then turned and briskly walked toward the street exit where he hailed a cab. As soon as he got into the back seat, Coop and Zoe came running and jumped in next to him. The taxi took off.

"Lots of cloak and dagger," Coop said. "What's up?"

"Mossad's been on my tail since you left. I'm giving them just enough to keep them interested, but when they get too close, ditch them. How was Iran?"

Coop opened his briefcase and handed Mac the records from the Tehran Office of Accounting. McNamara skimmed through the documents. "So who does the Luxembourg numbered account belong to?"

Coop took the papers and set them back in his case. "When we figure that out, we'll know who the bad guys are. I'm thinking of getting help from Mossad."

McNamara broke out laughing. "Yeah, sure. Blum's not going to walk the plank for you, if that's what you're thinking."

Coop took some time phrasing his answer. He knew it was going to antagonize Zoe. "I'm not sure we can trust Blum," he said.

Zoe's back stiffened. "What do you mean? He's the only one who's given us any help."

Coop patted her knee. "Take it easy. I'm just saying, I didn't buy his explanation for those guys showing up at the amusement park. Maybe he has his own agenda."

Zoe pushed Coop's hand away. "I trust him. One hundred percent."

"I get that, but this Mossad agent, Lev Cohen, he owes me. I saved his ass in Beirut. Let's give him a try and if we strike out there, we'll go back to David Blum."

"Whatever. You're the boss," Zoe said.

Coop pinched her cheek. "You look so cute when you pout."

~ * ~

McNamara had made a visit to Lev Cohen when Lev was recuperating from his Beirut gunshot wound, so when Mac phoned him and reintroduced himself, he was warmly received. McNamara asked if he could stop by and discuss a matter with him.

Lev invited him into the living room and poured a couple glasses of iced tea. "So, have you found your boss yet?" Lev asked.

Mac took a sip. "Well, you should know, your guys have been on my ass since I got here."

Lev chuckled. "I wouldn't know about that—not my department. So, what brings you here today?"

"Okay, I did find Coop. He's uncovered some interesting information, but he needs inside help to corroborate it. He seems to think you'll go out on a limb for him."

Lev used body language to make himself look as uncomfortable as possible. "I don't know. I don't think so."

"Coop says you owe him."

"Yes, I owe him, but not my career."

"All he's asking for is a meeting with you...to explain what he's dug up."

Lev did a little hemming and a little hawing before he said, "Okay, when and where?"

"Two o'clock, the carousel at Luna Park. I'll go with you."

~ * ~

It had turned cold and begun to rain. Coop and Zoe stopped at a nearby store and bought hooded raincoats.

They left their boutique hotel where they had found a room for sixty bucks a night, and grabbed a taxi to the park. They arrived at ten minutes of two. "Lev doesn't know I found you, so you're not in on the meeting," Coop said.

"So why am I here?"

"Just like our meeting with Blum, only you're the one at the ice cream stand this time. Lev will be with McNamara. If you don't spot anyone following them, start eating the ice cream and I'll know the coast is clear. If not, throw it into the trash."

Zoe wrapped the hood over her head and took up her sentry post. Coop stood next to the carousel ticket booth and rubbed his hands together to keep the blood circulating. At the moment the park clock chimed twice, Coop spotted McNamara and Lev Cohen getting out of a cab.

The rain had chased away most of the fun seekers; there was no crowd for a tail to hide behind. Coop did a quick three-sixty surveillance and glanced at Zoe who was doing the same. No one was within a hundred yards.

McNamara nudged Lev toward the ticket booth. Lev spotted Coop standing next to it and did his best to hide his excitement. He thrust out his hand. "Hey, Coop, you left my place without saying goodbye. Good to see you again."

Coop shook Lev's hand. "Yeah, sorry about that." He handed Lev a ticket. "Let's you and I take a ride on the merry-go-round."

They started toward the revolving amusement ride and Coop peeked over at the ice cream stand. Zoe was making a point of dumping a fudsicle into the garbage can. Coop looked around; other than McNamara, the park was still deserted.

Coop tapped Lev's arm. "Wait here a minute, I have to get something from McNamara." He jogged back toward Mac, but ran right past him. "It's blown," he said to him, as he took off running.

By the time Coop reached the taxi, Zoe was inside with the door open. Coop jumped in and the driver sped off.

"Who did you see?" Coop asked.

"Him."

"Him? Who's him?"

"The guy who came to my house. The guy who set up my meeting with Mizrahi."

Coop's eyes opened wide. "Lev? He's the guy who set the deal up?"

Zoe nodded. "He's the guy."

Forty-two

The cab dropped Coop and Zoe two blocks from their hotel and they walked the rest of the way. No one was following. Ten minutes later, McNamara knocked on the hotel room door and when Coop opened it, Mac just stared at him. "What was that?" he said.

"Zoe recognized Lev Cohen. He's the guy who set up the deal for her to wire the nine million to Mizrahi. I'm guessing he's also the one who paid off our wire transfer bandits."

McNamara took a miniature Irish whisky from the mini bar and drank it right out of the bottle. "Holy shit, so do you think he's the guy with the numbered account?"

"We're going to find out. Do you have your cell with you?"

Mac handed his phone to Coop who handed it to Zoe. "Ask her how you get back into a numbered account once it's set up."

Zoe dialed 00, then 41, the country code for Switzerland, then the cell number. A recording came on after five rings. *"This is Lara Graf. Vice President of Swiss Commerce Bank. Leave a message and I'll return your call."* Zoe left McNamara's number and told Lara to call her back as soon as possible.

Coop grabbed his raincoat. "Stay here and wait for her call. I'll be back in a couple hours."

The cab dropped Coop in front of the central bus station and he dodged hookers for three blocks on the way to Moses Rabinsky's private office. He rang the bell and knocked on the metal gate, but no one answered. He was sure Moishe was inside; the smell of boiling gefilte fish was seeping through the old wooden door. This time he rattled the metal back and forth.

The door opened a crack and Moishe's right eye peeked around it. "I already gave you the passports and the contact. Go away."

Coop held up a fistful of cash. "I need something else."

Moishe spotted the money and hurried to open the metal gate. "Come in, come in. A glass of Arak, maybe?"

"No, I'm good." Coop plopped a couple thousand dollars in bills on the table. "I need a drug that will knock a person out for a couple hours."

"Are you talking about GHB or Rohypnol?"

"Yeah, exactly."

Moishe lifted his brows. "Those are date rape drugs."

"Yeah, I know, but I don't need them for that purpose. Can you get one of them?"

Moishe straightened out the bills and placed them in piles as he counted them. "Two hundred more," he said.

Coop sighed and dropped four fifties on top of a pile. "And I want a syringe."

"Tomorrow at four o'clock."

Coop shook his head. "Uh, uh. Today by five o'clock."

"I cannot get it that fast."

Coop scooped up the money. "No problem, I'll talk to someone else."

Moishe grabbed at the bills. "Wait, wait. I didn't really mean I can't get it today."

"Oh, yeah? What did you mean?"

"I, uh...I mean I will have a vial of GHB by six."

Zoe was talking on Mac's phone when Coop got back to the room. "I can't promise you I'll be back," Zoe said. She listened for a response and said, "I'll let you know. Goodbye, Lara."

"You look like you need a drink," Coop said. He raided the mini bar and poured Mac and Zoe Irish whiskeys. He took a Jack Daniels for himself. "Relationship problems?" he said.

Zoe took a big gulp from the bottle. "Yeah, I don't know if it's worth it. Honestly, I think I'd just like to be back with the Agency sneaking up on bad guys."

"First things first. What did Lara say about getting into a numbered account?"

"She said if Luxembourg is anything like Switzerland, it takes an iris recognition match to the one they have on file."

~ * ~

It was after nine p.m. when Coop stepped into the lobby and approached the doorman who was seated behind a metal desk reading a newspaper. "I'm a friend of Mr. Cohen's. Could you ring him and see if he's in?"

The man didn't bother to look up from his paper. "He's not. saw him leave ten minutes ago."

Coop snapped his fingers. "Damn. I'll come back tomorrow." He stepped out the door and signaled Zoe to follow.

They went around to the back of the building where Coop used a key to enter the rear stairwell. Zoe took two stairs at a time to reach the eighth floor and was waiting for Coop when he finally got there—sucking in as much air as his good lung would hold. "Man, on one lung it's easier going down," he said.

The same key fit Lev's back door and they stepped inside his condo. The drapes were open and the lights from boats docked in the marina sparkled against the calm water. Coop opened the fridge and took out two beers. He handed one to Zoe and they sat in the dark drinking and waiting.

Around eleven-thirty, they heard a key jiggling in the front lock. They withdrew their Glocks and took positions on either side of the door. Lev stepped inside and two pistols pushed against his temples. "Just hold it right there," Coop said.

Coop kept his gun barrel pressed against the side of Lev's head while Zoe stripped him of his weapon. Then she yanked his arms behind his back and tightened a zip tie around his wrists. Coop re-holstered his pistol.

"How did you get in here?" Lev asked.

Coop smiled. "Spy rule number one. Never trust another spy with your house key."

Lev forced a smile. "I guess I should have changed the locks after you took off."

"I guess," Coop said.

"Okay, so what do you guys want?"

Zoe switched on the hall light to illuminate her face. "Do you recognize me?"

Lev shrugged. "Should I?"

"You came to my house with phony credentials and you set up a meeting for me with Mizrahi."

"Oh, yeah. You're that Fields chick."

Zoe laid her fist into Lev's midsection. "I'm not a Fields chick. I'm Zoe Fields with twenty-five years in the Agency and you're a Mossad agent in deep shit."

The breath was knocked out of Lev and he struggled to get words out. "I..I think it's the other way around. You and Coop are fugitives and when Mossad catches up with you, you're both going to prison for a long time."

Zoe cocked her arm to deliver another blow, but Coop stepped between them and nudged Zoe away. He stared at Lev. "Have you ever been to Luxembourg? At the Bank of Trade, maybe?"

The smug expression washed away from Lev's face. "Luxembourg? Maybe. Maybe on a case a few years ago, but I didn't know they even had a bank of trade. Why?"

"I think you were there a few weeks ago."

"Well, you think wrong."

"Let's head into your guest bedroom," Coop said.

"What? Why?"

"I remember you have a Hamilton safe in the closet. If you haven't been to Luxembourg lately, you won't mind opening it for us."

"That's not going to happen. My private stuff is in there and it's none of your business, so no way will I give you the combination."

"It doesn't need a combination. You told me it works off your thumbprint. Remember?"

"Well, you'll have to cut off my thumb then, because I'm not opening it for you."

Coop took a leather pouch and a jackknife from his pocket. He handed the knife to Zoe and removed a vial and a syringe from the pouch. He shoved the needle through the rubber top of the vial and sucked out 5 ccs of GHB, then he held the needle toward the ceiling and tapped the syringe several times to get rid of any air bubbles.

Lev's cavalier attitude disappeared and he tugged his wrists against the restraints. "What the fuck? Hey, let's talk about this." he said.

Coop wasn't in the mood for any type of negotiation. He jabbed the syringe through Lev's shirt into the fleshy part of his shoulder and deposited all of the drug into the muscle. It didn't take long before Lev's eyelids got heavy and he passed out.

Coop took one armpit, Zoe the other and they dragged Lev into the extra bedroom closet. "Drop him in front of the safe," Coop said.

Lev's limp body sagged to the floor. Zoe extended the blade of the knife and cut the zip tie from Lev's wrists. The safe had a one-inch circular glass window. Coop stretched Lev's right hand to it and pressed his thumb against it. Nothing happened. He grabbed Lev's other hand and used his left thumb. A small green indicator lit up and the safe emitted a clicking sound. Coop turned to Zoe. "You want to do the honors?"

Zoe turned the handle and opened the safe. It was stuffed with documents, a few bundles of cash and a plastic bag. She discarded the money and the bag and started through the papers. There was a car registration, a deed to the condo, six or seven insurance policies and a couple passbooks for local banks. On the bottom of the clutter was a letter with the heading: **Luxembourg Bank of Trade** and in between the boiler plate sentences were the numbers, **HZ530-247-9555**.

Zoe handed Coop the letter and he neatly folded it and slipped it into his pocket. "What's in the plastic bag?" he asked. Zoe peeled it open and turned it upside down. A box cutter, with dried blood stains all over the blade, fell out.

Forty-three

Rachel Kagan knew Lev Cohen wanted more than a business relationship and she was willing to lead him on, so long as it was advantageous to her. It looked like they were getting close to apprehending Craig Cooper; he had reached out to Lev. Once Cooper was charged with Mizrahi's murder and she had her half of the nine million dollars, she would tender her resignation and disappear to the Bahamas or Caymans or some other safe exotic place like that.

Lev's meeting with Cooper had been scheduled for two o'clock this afternoon, but Lev never let Rachel know how it went. She called his cell a couple times and each time it transferred to voicemail.

It was past midnight and Lev still hadn't called, so she dialed his number one more time. She received the same recording: *This is Lev Cohen. Leave a message.*

Rachel left another message. "Dammit Lev, I miss you, honey. Give me a call. I need to know how this afternoon went and whether you disposed of that item I gave you. I'll be up all-night waiting for your call."

Forty-four

Lev was still out cold. Coop relieved him of his cell and was n the process of calling C.T. when the phone buzzed. He let it go o voicemail and after listening to Rachel's message he completed he call to his pilot.

A sleepy voice answered. "Yeah? Who is it?"

"It's me, Coop. Listen, C.T., get the plane and crew ready for a trip to Luxembourg."

"When?"

"In about six hours. Zoe and I will be on a commercial flight hat gets into Cyprus at five a.m. As soon as we get there, we'll have a van drop us at the Gulfstream."

"Okay, I'll file a flight plan."

"Perfect and by the way, we'll be taking a sick patient on the light, so have a seat made into a bed."

"Gotcha."

Coop glanced over at the couch where Lev was waking up from his stupor. His eyes would open and then they would slowly close and then they would open and then they would close again.

Coop looked at Zoe. "Better get him some water, he's going to be pretty dehydrated."

When Lev was able to keep his eyes open for more than thirty seconds, he began to mumble. Zoe put the water bottle to his mouth and squirted a few drops onto his tongue. He opened and closed his lips like a newborn looking for a nipple.

Coop used Lev's phone and tapped in McNamara's number. He answered on the first ring. "That you, Coop?"

"Yeah, did you get all the stuff?"

"Got it."

"Great. Zoe will meet you out front in twenty minutes."

Lev began to moan and Zoe went to check him out. His eyes had closed again and she had to use her fingers to open the lids. The whites had disappeared and were replaced by a dark pink color. "He doesn't look very good," she said.

Coop came over to take a peek. "Yeah, you're right, but we have no choice. If he comes around on the plane, he gets another shot."

Zoe went down the back stairs and met Mac, who was waiting near the alley. He was dressed in blue hospital scrubs and holding on to a wheelchair and a blanket. He handed Zoe a matching pair of scrubs. "Hope you're a size three."

Zoe laughed. "I haven't been a three since I was twenty." She stripped off her jeans and shirt and squeezed into the scrubs.

Mac raised his eyebrows. "Makes your boobs look bigger."

Zoe shook her head. "Another goddamn boob guy."

McNamara led the way and Zoe followed with the wheelchair as they entered through the front door. The night doorman held up his hand and began to speak in Hebrew. Mac said, "Sir, English please, I'm from the British hospital. What floor is Mr. Lev Cohen on?"

The flustered attendant scrolled quickly through the occupant list. "Eight, eight-o-two. Is he all right?"

"We'll let you know." He and Zoe stepped into the elevator.

Coop was waiting at the front door and took his set of scrubs from under the blanket. He tossed his street clothes next to the blanket and slipped into the hospital uniform. "The taxi is here. Help me get him into the chair," Coop said.

Lev was beginning to stir once again and was mumbling incoherent sentences. They strapped him into the wheelchair and put the blanket over his lap and legs. Coop and Zoe pushed the chair ahead of them and headed to the elevator; Mac slipped out through the back staircase. When the doors opened on the main floor, Coop hustled Lev out the front entrance. Zoe turned to the doorman. "He'll be fine," she said.

They lifted Lev out of the wheelchair and stuffed him into the back seat of the taxi. Zoe sat next to him and Coop rode up front. The cab dropped them in front of the Aegean Airlines terminal where they strapped Lev back in the chair and Coop checked them on to the flight. Coop had searched through Lev's phony passport drawer and pulled out his German one. He was boarded as Gunther Schmidt from Hamburg.

The flight only took fifty-five minutes. The doctor, nurse and patient were allowed to deplane first; they wheeled Lev up the jetway at five minutes after five.

The Gulfstream was attached to an auxiliary power unit, so when Coop, Zoe and Lev boarded, the cabin was bright and the temperature was warm. Josie, the flight attendant, was back on duty. "Good morning, sir," she said. "Breakfast?"

The direct flight distance from Cyprus to Luxembourg was seventeen hundred and nine miles and the flight time was three hours and five minutes. By the time C.T. set the Gulfstream on the runway at Findel Airport, Lev Cohen was awake and semi-alert. He looked at Coop. "Wh...where are we? What are you doing with me?"

Coop strapped a new zip tie on Lev's wrists and moved in close. "We're in Luxembourg. Can you guess why?"

Lev spit in Coop's face. "You'll never get the money."

Coop wiped his cheek with a napkin. "Yeah, we'll see about that. Won't we?"

Forty-five

Rachel Kagan was worried. She had called Lev six times and each time the call reverted to voicemail. She slammed the door to her apartment and hailed a cab.

It was always a mystery to her why Lev had chosen Frischmann Beach to buy his condo. It was saturated with people who felt entitled and who thought they were better than the other people in Tel Aviv. She always feigned indignance, but down deep she was jealous. "What does he need with another four and half million," she muttered under her breath.

The doorman recognized Rachel immediately and tipped his hat. "Good evening, Ms. Kagan. You're quite late tonight."

"Good evening, Daniel. Do you know if Mr. Cohen is at home?"

The doorman shrugged. "I just started my shift at three, so I really don't know."

Rachel took the elevator to the eighth floor and sorted through the keys on her ring. Lev thought it was romantic for her to have a key to his apartment. She let him think she felt the same way.

As soon as she stepped inside, she knew something was wrong. Lev was an obsessive-compulsive when it came to cleanliness, but there were empty beer bottles on the coffee table and a couple pharmacy wrappers wadded up on the carpet.

She raced to the extra bedroom and threw open the closet door. The door to Lev's safe was ajar and the papers inside were disheveled. She sorted through them, looking for the one document of value—the letter from the Luxembourg Bank of Trade. It was gone.

It hadn't crossed Rachel's mind that Lev might double-cross her, but he was missing and so was the bank letter. It wasn't rocket science to conclude that Lev had gone for the money without her. The only encouraging discovery of the evening was the absence of the box cutter; hopefully it was at the bottom of the Yarkon River.

She Googled the Luxembourg Bank of Trade and dialed their phone number. The recorded message said the bank would open at eleven a.m. It was four here, but Luxembourg was an hour behind Tel Aviv, so it was only three there. If she was lucky and could get a flight in the next hour, she could be at the bank when it opened.

Forty-six

The pilots and the flight attendant were sitting in the rear of the passenger compartment having breakfast. Coop joined them. "Any idea when stores open around here?" Coop asked.

C.T. looked over at the flight attendant. "Ask Josie, she's the shopper."

"Usually nine," she said.

"Could you do a little shopping for me?" Coop asked.

"Sure, what do you want me to buy?"

Coop handed Josie a piece of paper with a handwritten list: *Three-piece blue pinstripe suit, size 44 coat, 38 waist, 34 inseam. A white shirt 17/34. A red tie. Black shoes size 11½, black socks.*

Josie checked out the list. "Going to the prom, are ya?"

Coop laughed and handed her a fistful of hundreds. "Just get them here by ten o'clock, wise ass." He handed C.T. fifty dollars. "Pick up a duffel bag, will ya."

"How big?"

"Real big," Coop said.

As soon as the shoppers left on their errands, Coop called the terminal and arranged for a six-passenger disability van and a small sedan to be delivered to the Gulfstream by ten o'clock.

He stepped into the bathroom and peered into the mirror. His salt and pepper beard was scraggly, his gray hair was curling down the back of his neck and his eyes were bloodshot. He turned on the shower and let all the filth of the last few days wash down the drain. After he dried, he shaved off his beard and trimmed his hair; two doses of eye drops cleared up his eyes.

The shoppers returned. C.T. held up the duffel and Josie handed Coop three large bags from the Ralph Lauren store. He patted her on the back and retreated to the bathroom. When he stepped out, he looked like a new man.

"Wow," Zoe said. "You lookin' for a date, big guy?"

Coop shook his head. "Another smart ass. Okay, listen up C.T. you're going to drive the van and I'll ride in back with Lev and his wheelchair. Oh, and make sure you wear your uniform. Zoe you follow in the car, but keep your distance." He turned to the copilot. "Have the Gulfstream ready to go…and I mean ready. Any questions?" Everyone looked to the person next to them. All heads were moving side to side.

"Okay." Coop turned to Zoe. "Let's get some weapons out of the safe."

At ten o'clock Coop looked through the window of the plane. The vehicles were parked side by side next to the Gulfstream. He motioned to Zoe. "Give me a hand with Lev."

They walked up the aisle to the seat Lev was occupying. The drugs had completely worn off and he was agitated. He was screaming obscenities and banging his restrained hands against the armrests. Coop removed the syringe from its pouch and filled it with another 5ccs of the GHB drug. Zoe grabbed Lev's arm and twisted it until he felt it would pop from its socket. Coop jabbed the needle into his shoulder, but only injected a half dose into Lev' arm. His eyes closed and his head slumped. Coop replaced the syringe, still containing a half dose, into the pouch.

It took all three of them to get Lev strapped into the wheelchair and down to the tarmac. C.T. lowered the van's ramp and Coop pushed the wheelchair into the back. Before he closed the doors he turned to Zoe. "Remember, keep your distance and if anything looks suspicious, call me on this cell." He handed her a new burner phone. "The number is on the speed dial."

It took twenty minutes to reach the financial district where the Luxembourg Bank of Trade was located. There was no mistaking it—a holdover from the nineteenth century surrounded by twenty-first century architecture. C.T. parked in a handicap zone, ten feet from the entrance.

Coop waited for the clock in the bank's tower to strike eleven and when the chiming stopped, he opened the rear doors of the van and wheeled Lev down the ramp and into the bank. He scanned the marble floored room for the man he thought would be most senior. He picked out an older gentleman with a bald head and a short moustache. His nameplate read: Wilhelm Weber.

He wheeled Lev to the side of the desk and handed the executive his Canadian passport along with Lev's German one. "Mr. Weber...I am Bernard Martin. I am the financial conservator for Mr. Gunther Schmidt." He pointed to the wheelchair.

Wilhelm stood and offered his hand. "So very nice to meet you sir. May I be of service today?"

"I believe so. Mr. Schmidt has a numbered account here at the Bank of Trade and he wishes to close his account."

Weber stroked his moustache. "Well, as I am sure you are aware, it is not necessary for me to be present when a numbered account is accessed. After verifying that Mr. Schmidt is the owner of the account, a withdrawal can be transferred by any of my staff."

"Indeed, I am quite aware of that," Coop said. "However, my advice to Mr. Schmidt is to take this withdrawal in cash."

"I see...and how much is the withdrawal for?"

"Nine million dollars."

Weber thought for a moment. After forty years with the bank, he had witnessed cash withdrawals for much more than this one. "I don't see this as a problem," he said. He glanced down at Lev. A couple drops of saliva were escaping his lips. "If I may ask, what is Mr. Schmidt's medical problem?"

"Diabetes followed by a stroke two months ago. That's why I was brought in by Mr. Schmidt's family to make financial decisions for him."

"That's too bad. Yes, quite a pity."

"May we get on with the verification process?" Coop asked.

"Yes, yes, by all means. Do you have the number?" Coop handed him the letter taken from Lev's safe.

Weber stepped away from his desk and waved his hand in the direction of a private room. "Please, follow me."

The 2.5 ccs were beginning to wear off and Lev lifted his head and babbled out a few words. Coop leaned down and whispered part of the English alphabet into Lev's ear. Lev's head swayed slightly and he yelled out a few obscenities. "Yes, Gunther, Mr. Weber is quite competent," Coop said out loud.

Coop looked at the banker. "It doesn't appear so, but he's very aware of the proceedings." He pushed the wheelchair and followed Weber into the adjoining room.

Weber sat down at a computer and typed in the numbers of the account. Two red lights appeared on a companion computer. "Can he open his eyes?" Weber asked. "I will need an image of each one."

Coop rolled the wheelchair as closely as he could to the computers. Then, he gently used his thumb and index finger to separate the upper and lower lids of Lev's right eye.

Weber picked up a scope that was hard wired to the computer displaying a graphic of the human eye on its screen. He placed the scope in front of Lev's eyeball, pulled a trigger and the device performed a scan in less than ten seconds. A light on the computer screen turned from red to green. "And the left one please," Weber said.

Coop touched Lev's left lid. Both his eyes opened wide and he threw his head back. "Who's got my money, goddammit?" he shouted.

Coop patted Lev on the shoulder and turned to Weber. "Please excuse Mr. Schmidt. As you can see, he is anxious to get his money, but he ate just before we came here and I suspect his glucose level must be quite high. If you don't mind, I'll inject some insulin."

"By all means," Weber said.

The syringe still contained 2.5 ccs of the GHB drug and Coop emptied into Lev's arm. Lev mumbled an incoherent sentence and Coop put his ear to Lev's lips. "Yes, you'll get your money. Now close your eyes and rest." Lev passed out again.

Coop went through the lid procedure with Lev's left eye and the second light also turned green.

"Very good," Weber said. He handed Coop a printed piece of paper. "After you fill out this withdrawal form, we can proceed to the vault. How do you propose to transport the cash?"

"I'll have my man bring in a case." Coop dialed C.T.'s cell. Five minutes later, the chauffeur, dressed in a pilot's uniform, set a duffel next to the wheelchair.

Weber called for an assistant to help him and then turned to Coop. "Follow me, please," he said.

Coop fell in line pushing the wheelchair, and C.T. followed carrying the duffel. The door to the main vault was open, but another door leading to a secondary strong room was shut and secured by a lock and a large spoked wheel. Weber punched several numbers on a keyboard, spun the wheel and tapped in a few more numbers. After a third input, he pushed down on a large handle and the door opened. When Coop stepped into the secondary vault, he noticed the steel walls were over a foot thick.

Weber began handing ten-thousand-dollar bundles to the assistant, who counted them in front of Coop and then placed them into his duffel. It was obvious the process was going to take close to an hour.

Forty-seven

Rachel caught a late Lufthansa red eye at four-fifty a.m. It landed at ten-ten in Luxembourg. She stopped to retrieve the weapon she had surrendered when boarding and dropped it into her briefcase, then headed straight to the car rental kiosk.

The Luxembourg Bank of Trade was listed in the Audi's GPS as an historical building; all she had to do was tap the 'go to' icon. At ten forty-five, she slipped into a parking slot across the street from the bank and waited for it to open.

At five minutes to eleven, Rachel spotted a van pulling into a handicap zone in front of the building. She opened her briefcase, took out a set of binoculars and focused them on the van. At eleven o'clock the rear doors opened and a well-dressed man in a three-piece suit pushed a wheelchair down the ramp.

The guy looked familiar, but Rachel couldn't quite place him. She fine-tuned the field glasses to sharpen the image. His beard was gone and his hair was cut short, but there was no mistaking him. "Welcome to Luxembourg, Deputy Cooper," Rachel said. She tried to focus in on the patient in the chair, but it was impossible to get a good look when Cooper turned to enter the bank. Even so, she was quite certain it was Lev Cohen in the wheelchair.

Rachel hadn't seen a driver leave the van, so she held her position and waited. About twenty minutes later, a uniformed man stepped out of the driver's door carrying a duffel and hustled into the bank. When the bank door closed behind him, she screwed silencer onto her pistol and headed for the van.

She tried the doors, but they were locked. The rear ones where Coop had come out with the wheelchair, were protected by a single keyhole. Rachel leveled her pistol and put three shots through it. The lock imploded. She looked around to see if anyone was looking her way and when she was confident no one was, she opened the back door and crawled inside the van.

Zoe was parked fifty yards away and watched the entire event unfold. She took out the burner and tapped in Coop's name on the speed dial. A computerized voice answered. *"The party you are trying to reach is not available."* She dialed it two more times and got the same message.

Zoe gave it some thought for a moment. She hadn't recognized the woman who entered the van, so the woman probably wouldn't recognize her either. She tucked her pistol under her shirt and strolled along the sidewalk toward the bank.

A bench and a newspaper rack were located on the sidewalk near the bank's front doors. She pretended to place a coin in the slot, took a paper from the pile and sat down on the bench. The paper was written in French, so she didn't understand a word, but she looked very intent as she leafed through the pages.

Forty-five minutes passed and Zoe was on her third trip through the news. She glanced up at the van. She couldn't see through the dusty windows, but she was certain the woman was watching. The bank doors opened and she heard Coop's voice say "Thank you, thank you so much, Mr. Weber. Have a nice day."

As soon as Zoe had a visual on Coop, C.T. and the wheelchair she made a dash toward them. "Leave him, leave him here." She pointed up the street. "Get to the car."

Coop didn't ask for an explanation. He let go of the wheelchair, grabbed C.T. by the arm and they took off running. C.T. was in great shape and managed to keep up even with a hundred and thirty pounds of cash slung over his shoulder.

Rachel saw her fortune getting away and flung the van's doors open. She put C.T. in her sight and fired. He went down. Now Zoe had an unobstructed view of Rachel and fired three times. Rachel toppled out of the van onto the blacktop.

Coop heard the discharge from Zoe's gun and turned around. C.T. was on the ground with blood oozing through his white flight shirt just below the left epaulet. Zoe ran past them, started the car and jumped it onto the curb next to C.T. He was holding on to his shoulder. "I'm okay," he said.

"Get in the back seat," Coop yelled. C.T. did as he was told and Coop followed him in.

Zoe tried to lift the duffel, but it was too heavy. She grunted and dragged it onto the passenger seat, then ran around to the driver's side and sped off.

Coop stripped the shirt off C.T.'s left arm. The flesh of his biceps was hanging out of the skin like a piece of steak butchered with a butter knife. "It doesn't look that bad," Coop said.

C.T. snuck a peek and rolled his eyes. "Yeah, it looks great."

"I'm just saying, you don't have to see a doctor...yet."

Zoe pulled up next to the Gulfstream and slammed on the brakes. C.T. wanted to help with the duffel, but Coop sent him up the stairs and he and Zoe lugged the bag on board. Before the door was latched shut, the copilot had the jet engines humming and in five minutes he was taxiing out for takeoff.

Forty-eight

After the Gulfstream reached cruising altitude, Coop made his way to the cockpit. He looked at C.T. Josie had cleansed and dressed his left arm and a clean shirt covered the bandage. "Hey, buddy, how're ya doing?" Coop said.

"I'm running out of Advils, but I'm fine. Hey, why are we headed to Limassol instead of Larnaca?"

"It's our last day in the Mediterranean. I thought we'd spend it at a resort I stayed at a lifetime ago."

"Sounds great."

"Yeah, well, you're going to spend it at the hospital, so don't get too excited."

The Amara hadn't changed since Coop was there a month ago. It was still luxurious, beautiful and still hosted by the same front desk crew. "Hey, Irv, how're doing?" Coop said.

The Brooklyn native looked around to make sure no one else heard the greeting. "Please, Mr. Wainwright. It's Basil, Basil Nightingale."

"Whoops, forgot. So, Basil, I need five rooms overlooking the sea."

Irv scrolled through a window of his computer. "I have a deal for you. Four rooms at nine-twenty apiece and the fifth room at half price."

Coop was in no mood to haggle. "Sounds good."

When they were all settled in their rooms, Coop called a taxi and sent C.T. to the hospital. Everyone else bought bathing suits from the hotel boutique and met around the pool for drinks.

A tanned young woman dressed in shorts and high heels approached to take their orders. "What does a Cypriot drink on a beautiful day?" Coop asked.

The woman smiled wide, her white teeth contrasting against her olive skin. "I would say a brandy sour?"

"We'll have four of those," Coop said.

No one was in the mood for chit-chat, so they stretched out on loungers and sipped their drinks. In a half hour the cocktail waitress stopped by. "Another round?" she asked.

"What's in those things?" Zoe said. "They're delicious."

"It's very much the national drink of our country: a mix of Cypriot brandy, undiluted lemon squash, a few drops of Angostura bitters, and then topped off with soda water."

Zoe looked at her fellow comrades; their glasses were empty. "Four more," she said.

They were finishing the round when C.T. walked onto the tiled patio surrounding the pool. He was wearing a bathing suit and his left arm had a new dressing and was resting in a sling. "What are you guys drinking?" he said.

Another round was ordered, but Coop and Zoe declined. They had more work to do and headed upstairs to Coop's room. "Do you still have Blum's number?" Coop asked.

Zoe looked through a notepad covered with her scribbling. "Yeah, I have it right here...somewhere."

"Love your filing system," Coop said.

"Whatever. Oh, here it is. Do you want me to do the talking?"

"He's your guy. I think you should."

Zoe tapped in his number. He answered on the third ring with the shortest salutation he could muster. "Blum."

"David, this is Zoe."

"Jesus Christ, Zoe, where the hell are you?"

"I'm in Cyprus with Coop and his crew. You better sit down and listen really well to what I'm going to tell you, because when you relate it to Halevi you'll probably get a promotion."

"Oh, Zoe, always a flair for the dramatic."

"This is drama all right, real life drama. Do you want to hear it or should I call the newspapers instead?"

"Okay, don't get huffy. Let's hear it."

Zoe took a deep breath and settled into a wicker chair. "First of all, we're sending you a box cutter in a plastic bag. It has fingerprints on the handle and blood on the blade. After you test it, we're pretty sure you'll find they're Rachel Kagan's prints and Abraham Mizrahi's blood."

"Whoa, whoa, are you saying Rachel killed Mizrahi?"

"That's exactly what I'm saying. Rachel brought Coop to the prime minister's residence for a meeting with Mizrahi, and Mossad thinks Coop was the last one to see him alive, but that's not true. After Coop's meeting, Rachel encouraged Coop to look around the grounds of the residence before heading back to Tel Aviv. During the forty-five minutes he was gone, Rachel must have snuck back to the room Mizrahi was in and she slit his throat."

"What? Why?"

"For nine million dollars. The nine million dollars I'm accused of sending to Iran." There was silence from Blum's end. "David, are you still there?"

"I'm still here, but I'm trying to catch my breath. Tell me about the money."

"Lev Cohen and Rachel Kagan found out about the money when you contacted Halevi to set up a meeting for me with Mizrahi. What you didn't know was that Halevi didn't arrange the meeting imself. He asked Lev to do it. And instead of getting the money to Mizrahi, Lev and Rachel decided to take it for themselves."

"Wait, wait. I saw a document that proved it was sent to Iran."

"Yeah, but it didn't stay there long. It ended up in a Luxembourg numbered account belonging to Lev Cohen. We'll end you the paper trail."

"I still don't get why Rachel would kill Mizrahi."

"She must have panicked. When she realized Coop was going o meet with him, she knew it was only a matter of time before Mizrahi figured out the scam. We don't think Lev had any idea she was going to kill Mizrahi, but we doubt he shed any tears over it."

"Okay, I think I get it. Where do we pick them up?"

"Send a team to Luxembourg and have them check all the hospitals and morgues. You'll find them."

"Zoe, I have a confession to make."

"Yeah? What's that?"

"After our second meeting, I began to question your innocence. 'm sorry."

"Apology accepted. Stay well, buddy, maybe we'll meet up again sometime." Zoe turned off her phone.

Coop stepped onto the balcony and Zoe joined him. They gazed out over the Mediterranean. The deep blue water shimmered from he reflection of the sun and as the waves broke near the beach the color of the water turned green. "Prettier than a postcard," Coop said.

Zoe closed her eyes and let the warm breeze bathe her face. "Maybe you should bring your family here someday."

"It would be nice, but Josh is a teenager now. He doesn't want o hang out with his mom and dad."

"Don't be so sure."

Coop broke from his brief trance. "Hey, do you have McNamara's cell number?"

Zoe laughed. "I'm sure it's in my file drawer." She stepped back inside and returned with a piece of paper and a cell phone. "Here," she said.

Coop dialed the number and Mac picked up on the first ring
"McNamara, who's calling?"

"Hey, Mac, it's Coop."

"Oh, man it's good to hear your voice. How did things go in
Luxembourg?"

"They worked out fine; I'll fill you in when we get back home
We're headed out tomorrow. Why don't you do the same."

"I will. See you at the office in a day or two?"

"Hey, Christmas is only three days away. Take some off
You earned it."

"Thanks, boss."

"No, thank you, Mac. Thanks for looking out for me."

Coop closed the phone and turned to Zoe. "A couple more
hours of sunlight. What say we join the group and get shit-faced?"

Forty-nine

The Gulfstream lifted off the Limassol runway a few minutes before ten a.m. After C.T. leveled off at thirty-two thousand feet, the flight attendant unbuckled her belt and stepped into the galley to prepare lunch. Coop called her back. "Josie, we just had breakfast. Sit down and enjoy the flight."

"I can't, sir. It's what I get paid for."

"Okay, I get it, but you have to follow one order."

"Sir?"

"Stop with the sir stuff. From now on, I'm just Coop."

She smiled widely. "Yes, sir...Coop."

Coop looked over at Zoe. She was in a pensive mood. "Penny for your thoughts," he said.

Zoe tried to smile, but the emotion wasn't there. "I hope I'm doing the right thing by not going back to Zurich."

"It's not too late. I can have C.T. divert to Switzerland."

"No, I'm going back to the States with you."

"What about Lara? Is it over?"

Zoe shook her head. "You know, as a V.P. of the bank, Lara's been involved with a lot of shady characters and she's done a few things that would stretch my code of ethics. I just can't stop wondering if she was somehow involved with the money going to Iran."

"What would have been her motive?"

"That's just it with her. You never know what's on her mind or, for that matter, what's on her agenda. I don't trust her, Coop, and if you can't trust the person you live with, you shouldn't be living with them."

"Then what's your plan?"

"The day after Christmas I'm going to march into Director Dutton's office, plop nine million dollars on his desk and ask for my job back."

"So you want to go back in the field?"

"I don't know, these last few weeks got my blood flowing. I loved it."

They sat without speaking for several minutes. Coop was the first to break the silence. "It got mine flowing too."

"So you're thinking of giving up the desk job?"

"I dunno. I promised Fran I wouldn't and I owe her for sticking with our marriage instead of just throwing in the towel. So, yeah, I'll have to think pretty hard about that."

They sat quietly, knowing the same thoughts were going through their minds. This time Zoe spoke up. "Will we make it home in time for you to get to Josh's game?"

Coop looked at his watch. C.T. had estimated a landing at Dulles at about three-thirty in the afternoon. "Yeah, I should," he said. "The game doesn't start till five."

Fifty

Neither Coop nor Zoe had slept very much over the last few weeks, so when Josie finished serving lunch, they both drifted off. Coop was the first to wake. He checked the time and couldn't believe it; he'd been out for five hours. He unbuckled his seatbelt and made his way to the cockpit.

C.T. turned around. "Hey, boss, what's up?"

"I just looked out the window and we haven't hit the coast yet. I figured we'd be descending by now."

C.T. sighed. "Yeah, sorry, I know you want to make your kid's game, but a cold front just dropped the minimums at Dulles, so we're going to have to line up and take our turn through the soup.'

Coop nodded. "I understand. What's the new ETA?"

C.T. looked at his GPS. "I'm shooting for four."

"Okay, I know you guys are going to be busy getting us on the ground, so I just want to thank you both now for what you did over there."

Both pilots waved their hands, and C.T. said, "All in the line of duty, boss. All in the line of duty."

"Hey, where's the satellite phone?" Coop asked.

C.T. opened a small cabinet. "It's here and it looks all charged; you can take it back to the cabin if you want." He handed it to Coop.

Zoe was still dozing; Coop took seat near the rear of the plane where he wouldn't wake her. He dialed in the long-distance codes and then his home number. Fran answered on the first ring. "Coop, is that you? Wainwright Construction came up on the I.D."

"Yeah, it's me. I'm on my way home."

"Oh, that's so great. When will you be here?"

"We'll land around four, so I'll head straight to the gym for Josh's game."

"He'll be so excited. Can I tell him?"

"Sure, and tell him there's no way in hell I'll miss this game."

"I will. I can't wait to see you. I've missed you."

"I've missed you too. See you in a couple hours."

Josie was securing all the loose items in the galley to prepare for landing. Coop called up to her. "Hey, Josie, thanks for everything."

Josie turned and waved. "It was my pleasure, Coop."

Zoe had wakened and Coop returned to join her. Twenty minutes later, C.T. lined up for the final approach. Coop and Zoe cinched their seat belts and Zoe put her hand on top of his. "You're thanking everybody and I never thanked you for coming to my rescue."

"After all the times you've saved my butt, you don't owe me any thank you."

"Well, I'm grateful. I'd forgotten how much I love working with you."

"Yeah, I love it too, but let's not get all mushy here. It's not like we'll never work together again."

Fifty-one

A wave of wintry D.C. air entered the plane as soon as the door was popped open. Coop spotted the black Escalade about twenty yards away from the Gulfstream and waved at the driver. He waved back and spun a U-turn to pull up next to the aircraft.

The driver stepped out. He was wearing a Washington Redskins ski cap over his head and ears and a scarf was wrapped around his face to protect his nose and mouth from the freezing temperature. He opened the tailgate and helped Zoe with the heavy duffel containing the cash and then gave Coop a hand with the other luggage.

Coop and Zoe jumped into the back seat and Coop leaned forward to give directions to the driver. "Drop me in Arlington and then take the lady downtown to the Club Quarters Hotel."

The driver raised his hand to signal he had gotten the message and then took off heading south. Coop was used to his drivers taking the shortest route, VA-267 East. He leaned forward again. "Which way are you going?" he asked.

The driver kept his eyes on the road and mumbled through his scarf. "Accident on 267. I'm taking I-66."

Coop knew that route was only a few minutes longer and leaned back in his seat to talk with Zoe. "You okay staying in a hotel? You're welcome to use our extra room."

Zoe laughed. "After those cheap hostels you put me up in, the Club Quarters is like the Ritz. Besides, you need some one-on-one time with your family."

"What about that sack full of money?"

"Don't worry, I'll sleep with it until I get it back to Dutton."

The driver took the next exit ramp and hung a right onto a deserted frontage road where he screeched to a stop. "What's the problem?" Coop said.

The driver pointed to the bottom corner of the dash. "The temperature gauge is going through the roof. I'll check the engine." He stepped outside and lifted the hood.

It was bitter cold out there and the driver appeared to be having a hard time bending under the hood. Coop and Zoe bundled up and stepped out of the car to help him. The driver lifted his head. The scarf he wore was pulled away from his face and in his right hand he held a German-made pistol with a silencer attached. He pointed it at Coop. "You should have given me an extra 10 ccs. I was on a plane out of Luxembourg before you even landed in Limassol."

"Yeah, well, I planned to, but my plan went south when your girlfriend showed up. How the hell did you know we went back to Cyprus?"

"It wasn't that hard to figure out. I am in the spy business you know."

Zoe's lips curled into a sneer. "So, what are you going to do now? Shoot two U.S. Agency operatives right in their own backyard?"

"Only one. You don't work for the Agency anymore."

Lev fired twice.

~ * ~

Coop slowly opened his eyes. He had an oxygen cannula under his nose, an IV in his left arm and his chest hurt where the surgeon had made his incision. A nurse wearing a surgical cap and mask patted him on the shoulder. "You're in Virginia Hospital," she said. "You're going to be all right."

Coop's eyes closed again, but he forced them open. "Zoe, where's Zoe?"

"She's still in surgery."

"Will she...will she make it?"

The nurse patted him again. "We'll see. You rest now. Your wife and son are waiting to see you."

Fifty-two

January was always the coldest month in Washington D.C. and 2011 was already on its way to being the coldest year. Ten inches of snow had fallen overnight and the roads were a mess, but Coop did what he had been doing every day for the last three weeks—visiting Zoe in the hospital.

Zoe had not regained consciousness following the operation and a few days ago the doctors decided to move her from the intensive care unit to the coma ward. Coop had developed a ritual that he went through at every visit. He would sit next to Zoe's bed, hold her hand and talk to her as if she could hear every word he was saying.

"Hey, Zoe, how're doing? I know I say this every day, but I'm sorry. Sorry I let you down. I should have recognized something wasn't right, but I was so anxious to get home, I dropped my guard. I fumbled the ball on the goal line. God, I'm so sorry."

He stood to leave and he gave Zoe's hand one last squeeze. He cocked his head; it almost felt like she squeezed back. He tightened his grip and so did she. "Zoe, are you there? Somewhere?"

Zoe's lids fluttered, but her eyes didn't open. "Zoe? Can you hear me?" Coop said.

Her grip relaxed but her lids continued to flutter and Coop was sure he saw her lips trying to move. "Come on Zoe, speak. Please, speak."

Coop stayed for another half hour, but nothing changed. He shook his head and reluctantly let go of her hand. He stepped to the door, but before he opened it, he turned around. "See you tomorrow," he said.

Meet Mike Paull

Mike Paull, a native of the San Francisco Bay Area, had two passions that preceded his writing career. He was a licensed dentist and a licensed commercial pilot. In 2000, he retired from dental practice, and in 2010, he retired from flying to embark on his new career.

His first book, *Tales from the Sky Kitchen Café*, is a series of short stories describing his experiences as a pilot hanging out in a small airport coffee shop. His next series of books, the *Brett Raven Mystery Trilogy*, features a dentist as the protagonist and mystery solver.

In 2021 Mike introduced, *Missing,* a spy thriller. *She's Missing,* is the second book in the *Missing* series.

Mike and his wife Bev now live two hundred miles north of San Francisco in Chico, CA.

Other Works from the Pen of

Mike Paull

Missing - A bullet to the back detours a government agent's search for a hidden stash of gold.

Letter to Our Readers

Enjoy this book?

You can make a difference

As an independent publisher, Wings ePress, Inc. does not have the financial clout of the large New York Publishers. We can't afford large magazine spreads or subway posters to tell people about our quality books.

But, we do have something much more effective and powerful than ads. We have a large base of loyal readers.

Honest Reviews help bring the attention of new readers to our books.

If you enjoyed this book, we would appreciate it if you would spend a few minutes posting a review on the site where you purchased this book or on the Wings ePress, Inc. webpages at:

https://wingsepress.com/

Thank You

Visit Our Website

For The Full Inventory
Of Quality Books:

Wings ePress.Inc
https://wingsepress.com/

Quality trade paperbacks and downloads
in multiple formats,
in genres ranging from light romantic comedy
to general fiction and horror.
Wings has something for every reader's taste.
Visit the website, then bookmark it.
We add new titles each month!

Wings ePress Inc.
3000 N. Rock Road
Newton, KS   67114

Made in the USA
Las Vegas, NV
16 September 2022

55424605R00128